THE *LITTLE* *B*LUE *H*OUSE

SANDRA COMINO

GROUNDWOOD BOOKS
DOUGLAS & McINTYRE
TORONTO VANCOUVER BERKELEY

Groundwood Books / Douglas & McIntyre
720 Bathurst Street, Suite 500, Toronto, Ontario M5S 2R4
Distributed in the USA by Publishers Group West
1700 Fourth Street, Berkeley, CA 94710

We acknowledge for their financial support of our publishing program the Canada Council for the Arts, the Government of Canada through the Book Publishing Industry Development Program (BPIDP), the Ontario Arts Council and the Government of Ontario through the Ontario Media Development Corporation's Ontario Book Initiative.

ONTARIO ARTS COUNCIL
CONSEIL DES ARTS DE L'ONTARIO

National Library of Canada Cataloging in Publication
Comino, Sandra
The little blue house / by Sandra Comino; translated by
Beatriz Hausner and Susana Wald.
Translation of: La casita azul.
ISBN 0-88899-503-2 (bound). –ISBN 0-88899-541-5 (pbk.)
I. Hausner, Beatriz II. Wald, Susana III. Title.
PZ7.C748Li 2003   j863'.7   C2003-901844-X

Printed and bound in Canada

The publishers regret that they have been unable to contact all copyright holders.

THE LITTLE BLUE HOUSE

To Cati, Marti, Gisela and Camila
To Agustín and Franco
And to Paloma and María

CONTENTS

THE LITTLE BLUE HOUSE

Saturday night. As usual, the whole town was getting ready to listen to the story on the radio. It had become a habit, although at first people had found the stories quite strange. It was always the same voice telling the stories, and the stories were always about the same thing.

Absolutely everybody would listen in. They would gather around the radio if they were at home or listen to a hand held radio if they were on the street.

The streetlight on the corner shone dimly. Someone wearing a long overcoat and a scarf tied in a knot below the chin hurried up to the radio station. The person opened the door and entered the building without a moment's hesitation, not stopping to take off either the scarf or the overcoat.

Immediately, the voice began to speak – the storytelling voice that was heard in homes all over the town.

LEGEND 1

Many years ago, before this town came to be, in a deserted land where the night was clean and clear, and not a breath of wind stirred the grass, an army of men massacred a group of natives. Spring had cooled the night air as though it were autumn. The tall grass held onto the dew until the morning, then drank it up when the sun came out.

Ailín lived happily in her camp, though her parents did not feel the same way. They still dreamed of living free in the open countryside, where they would not be constantly persecuted by European settlers. They dreamed of a peace that they feared they would never find again. They could never stay in the same place for long because the settlers always chased them away.

Aloe, Ailín's father, and Alma, her mother, dreamed of a better future for their daughter. They hoped that, in time, a native from their own village would come for her and together they would form a

THE LITTLE BLUE HOUSE

family. They also dreamed of the good dowry that Ailín would bring them one day.

Ailín, on the other hand, desired neither dowry nor marriage and dreamed only of living freely. She did not want to belong to any man. She wanted to live like a hare in the fields, or a dove in the air. She was sure of one thing – she would flee to the end of the earth if ever a man sang a love song in her ear. This was the way the men in her village courted the girls.

One night when the moon was full, a group of settlers burst into the camp. Armed to the teeth, they burned huts, abducted women and killed anyone who crossed their path. Aloe and his family and a few others fled blindly in terror, not even knowing where they were going. Such was the life of the natives whose lands had been taken over by the white people.

Once again, Ailín and her parents set out in search of a place where the air, the land and a home would belong to them, even if such a place did not exist.

They walked and they walked, until they thought that they had found that place.

A WINTER SUNDAY

It was nine o'clock on Sunday morning. Winter was coming to Azul, the town the world seemed to have forgotten, as it did every year. Azul greeted the cold weather with pleasure, knowing that its arrival was a law of nature. As the wind's brutal embrace took hold of the streets, an orange bus, driven by a woman, made its way down the main street.

At the same time, Cintia was heading out for her daily outing. Hat and backpack in hand, she got on her bicycle and pedaled down the dirt road. Careful not to be noticed – not very easy in such a small town – she turned onto the road that ran alongside the railroad tracks and followed it to the pond and her favorite secret hideaway – an abandoned house that, like all abandoned houses, had a long history.

Cintia often escaped to this place. She felt good

here. Ever since she was a little girl, she had heard mysterious rumors about the house and, because she was such a curious person, these rumors made her even more drawn to the secret place. She would make her way up the hill, cut a few little branches off the trees and spy through the windows, but she never managed to actually get inside.

Cintia left her bike next to the pump – the one you had to pump for twenty minutes before any water came out – and crossed the yard, looking carefully all around her. She fed crumbs to the pigeons that came to greet her and chased away the dogs that ran to the pond, scaring the flamingos.

She shooed away the lapwings that flew off, shrieking in her ear, and arrived at the pond. She walked along the water's edge past the weeping willows. Farther along the shore, she decided to wade in. The water came up to her ankles. She could feel how cold it was through her red rubber boots, and it was shallow enough that she could wade all the way out to a big rock that sat like a little island not far from shore.

She climbed up onto the rock and stretched out, leaning back on her elbows. Turning to look toward the town, she could see the hill near her own house, planted with *palos borrachos*. In March it was covered with pink blossoms. The hill where her best friend's house stood was covered in mimosa trees that turned yellow in August. The hill where the abandoned house stood was planted with jacarandas that bloomed sky-blue in November, though they had not yet flowered.

Cintia lay down on the rock and enjoyed the silent breeze – a silence broken only by the sounds of the lapwings, frogs and a few crickets.

Suddenly, a sound startled her. A flock of birds flew out of the pigeon loft, and the earth shook. She sat up and looked around. She saw no one, but something wasn't right. When birds flew away all at once, it was usually because something had disturbed them. Cintia wasn't afraid, but she knew that if the mayor found her in this place, it wouldn't be easy to explain what she was doing there.

Once again, she looked around to make sure that she was really alone. She took off her boots, shook out the water and left them to dry in the sun.

Doves continued to fly out of the pigeon loft. She looked over at the house again, at the pump, the swing, the cracks in the wall…

Nothing. Finally, she lay down and closed her eyes.

I've been coming here long enough. It's about time I stopped paying attention to imaginary noises, she thought to herself.

She lay still, so still that the silence became her own once again. The sky looked so big from where she was lying. Clouds swung overhead, turned and moved on toward other towns.

Many minutes went by. She closed her eyes and fell asleep. She'd been up late the night before, eager to finish the new novel Don Simón had lent her.

Suddenly, something tickled her nose. She was on her feet in a second.

"A bug!" she cried.

But it wasn't a bug. Someone was tickling her with a little jacaranda branch.

"I knew I'd find you here. Did I scare you?"

"Not at all," said Cintia, but she jumped off the rock and walked away so quickly that her pants were splashed with water.

It was her friend Bruno, who knew very well that he had frightened her, even though she'd never admit it. He was carrying a slingshot and had come to the pigeon loft to hunt for birds.

Bruno and Cintia were in seventh grade together, and they had been friends since kindergarten. They both loved this abandoned house on the outskirts of the town. They had heard all the rumors about it, as they were frequently discussed in town. They also knew how afraid everyone was of this forbidden place.

But all these secrets just piqued their curiosity even more. They were especially anxious to see what was inside the house. As far as they knew, no one in the town had ever even tried to get in!

They stood together on the shore and looked at the house. There was obviously a great secret hidden inside its four walls. But what was even more mysterious was something that happened to the house. It was something so strange that nobody in town could explain it, but so amazing that everyone looked forward to it.

Every November 28, as soon as everyone in Azul woke up, before they had even eaten breakfast, they all rushed over to the house to see if it had happened again. The mystery grew bigger year by year.

Bruno and Cintia were just pulling on their socks when the birds and the dogs announced the arrival of a car down the road. They grabbed the boots they had left to dry and waded back into the pond barefoot. They hid behind the rock, crouching down in the freezing water.

Cintia shivered with cold. Bruno put his arm around her shoulders. This made her shiver even more. She loved it when he hugged her. It gave her a funny feeling in her stomach.

Cintia could feel Bruno breathing. She was afraid that he could hear her heart beating.

"Hush," said Bruno. It felt like a scene out of one of the novels Cintia borrowed from Don Simón. Bruno let go of her. He needed both hands to get the slingshot out of his pocket, so he set down the boots he'd been holding. Then he put his arm around her once again while her heart kept racing wildly.

The black car made its way down the road. Some strangers got out, also in black. They approached the house but did not go in. Nor did they open the doors. They just talked among themselves and peeked in through the keyhole.

Ten minutes later they hung a metal sign on the door. Something was written on it, but Bruno and Cintia could not see what it was. Finally the people got back in the car and drove off. They hung another sign on the gate by the main road. Then they disappeared.

Bruno and Cintia stood up and waded out of the pond. He held his slingshot in one hand and their boots in the other. As far as Cintia was concerned, the slingshot was her friend's only shortcoming. If he wasn't so obsessed with hunting animals, everything would be perfect, she thought for the thousandth time.

Together they went up to the sign. FOR SALE, it read.

"For sale? It can't be!"

They looked at one another.

"Now we've really got to get in!"

"But we can't, not now. It's almost ten and I have to change and then go to the station to pick up the newspapers. Besides, Grandmother is expecting me for lunch," said Cintia, slipping her boots over her wet stockings.

"You're right. We can't stay now. But we can't wait until next Sunday, either. Why don't we come back this afternoon?" Bruno asked, as he helped Cintia with her bike.

"What if it isn't safe?"

Bruno thought for a few seconds.

"If we come before the mayor's wife gets here there won't be any danger. Everyone takes a nap on Sunday afternoon."

Their pants were soaking wet. They rode down the grassy lane that ran from the house to the gate where the other FOR SALE sign hung. Then they followed the dirt road back to town.

They were freezing!

The winter air tried to dry their wet clothes, but it just made them feel colder. Cintia sped up, crossed the railway tracks and disappeared into the distance. Bruno stopped and sat by the roadside to think.

VISITORS

Every Sunday, the orange bus took people out to the cemetery, a ten-kilometer ride down the road that led to the nearest big city. The mayor's wife drove the bus. It was her job to promote tourism in the town of Azul.

In places like Azul the townspeople aren't always happy with the decisions the mayor makes, but it is hard for them to stand up to him. People who hold positions of power usually get rich. The more money they make, the more powerful they become. It's difficult to resist this kind of authority, but not impossible. There are always people willing to take a stand.

Just like Cintia, the other children in Azul made secret visits to the abandoned house, eager to find out more about it. This put the mayor in a foul mood. To punish them, he would fine the families that allowed their children to go into the territory he had staked out for himself. It would be even worse for Cintia if she got caught, because the mayor was a friend of her father's. If her father found out that she was visiting that forbidden place, things would get very complicated indeed.

The mayor, Don Eduardo Ruverino, had a very important reason for protecting this secret place so zealously. Every Sunday afternoon at six o'clock sharp and immediately after her afternoon nap, Doña Hilda Ruverino led a guided tour for anyone interested in seeing the house from the outside. She would tell them bits and pieces of the legend of the abandoned house so that the visitors would go away intrigued.

Without a doubt, the abandoned house was being exploited by the mayor as if it were the town's heritage. No one knew who really owned the house, even though everyone knew the story of the owner's ancestors.

After each guided tour the mayor's wife would take visitors back to the tourist office, urging them to come back to Azul and promising to show them the inside of the house if they visited again. Of course, she never kept her promise.

Don Eduardo owned the hotel next to the railway station, where out-of-towners who visited Azul on Sundays would stop to have lunch before their tour of the abandoned house. Then they would walk around the jacaranda-covered hills and the pond, and hear about the love story that had taken place there so long ago.

But the story of the abandoned house was not the only thing the politicians took advantage of. Don Eduardo also charged townspeople one peso for a trip to the cemetery, though he used both the orange bus and his wife's services as bus driver for free. And because everyone in the village had a family member buried there, the sign-up sheet for cemetery visits on Sunday morning was always full, guaranteeing that the bus would be crammed with people. On important holidays there were even more people, so the orange bus made many trips back and forth to the cemetery.

In November and during the winter break, visits to the abandoned house also doubled. The promise that the mayor would reveal what lay inside the house provided a big incentive for many visitors to come back a second time.

As if this mystery were not enough, there was something else about the abandoned house that made Azul famous in the region. This mysterious, almost magical event repeated itself year after year and was very important to the mayor and his wife, as it brought great profit to the authorities of Azul. They took it upon themselves to spread the news of the annual happening, which had taken place every

November 28 since the oldest people could remember.

So November meant not only increased visits to the cemetery for the Day of the Dead celebrations, but also increased profits for Azul's very own feast day, held to celebrate the town's mysterious annual event.

Every year on November 28, the abandoned house – the house whose doors had remained shut for years and years – underwent an overnight change as momentous as someone whose skin changes color after too much exposure to the sun. The house would change color in the moonlight, and suddenly and without explanation, its white walls would turn completely blue.

Every November 27 the whole town attended the celebrations held on the eve of the house's color change. No one in Azul had actually witnessed the exact moment when the house changed from white to blue, which made things even more mysterious, because no one knew exactly when the change would take place, and when it would change back again. For the blue walls lasted only for one day.

The day before the mysterious change, the jacaranda celebrations began with an early-morning mass followed by the procession of Our Lady of the Rosary, as well as a dance where a queen and princesses were chosen. Queens from neighboring towns were also invited to attend the dance.

The most important event took place after these festivities. At dawn the next day, while everyone in Azul was still sleeping off the party from the previous day, the little abandoned house turned blue. This was the reason why, despite the fact that the rest of the year the house remained white, everyone referred to it as the little blue house.

THE TRAIN STATION

S unday, almost noon. The orange bus was on its way back from its usual trip to the cemetery. Cintia and Bruno had changed. Cintia had hidden her wet clothes at the bottom of the laundry basket – easier than having to explain why they were wet.

The Sunday train was due to arrive in Azul, and everyone was gathering at the station. The train-whistle announced to the town that it was eleven-thirty. Bruno rang his bicycle bell at Cintia's house so that she would come out, and they hurried off.

Meeting the train was a weekly event for the people of Azul. Children played in the station wait-ing room, women strolled together up and down the platform, and the men stood around in groups talk-ing about soccer.

The engine approached the station, blowing smoke and making loud noises to scare away the dogs and the hens wandering between the rails. Everyone stopped to look at the travelers who stared back at the locals with the same curiosity. Some of the passengers got off the train and went directly to the mayor's inn for lunch. The visitors only had one way to return home – the 11 P.M. train. Since the new president had ordered cutbacks, the train only came through Azul on Sundays. This was also the only day when people who didn't own cars could go to the big city.

The Sunday train provided another cause for excitement: the arrival of the weekly newspaper.

Cintia stopped by to see Manolito, who was in charge of the newsstand. She asked for two copies – one for her grandmother and another for her father. Manolito, however, would only sell one copy at a time, so Cintia had to stand in line twice. Bruno bought one for his mother. Then, laughing wildly, the two rode off on their bicycles, racing down the main street to see who would get to Cintia's house first.

The morning quickly filled up with the usual Sunday activities. By noon Azul was flooded with music coming from loudspeakers set up in the mayor's truck. The sound of *cumbias* filled the air, making everyone in town happy for a little while.

The orange bus was on its way back to the garage, and the townspeople were walking home to read the paper when suddenly, an imposing voice rang out over the music on the loudspeakers.

"Ladies and gentlemen of the town of Azul, guests and neighbors. As is our custom every Sunday, we invite you to join us for a tour of the little blue house. Only one peso! The orange bus will leave city hall at 6 P.M. sharp, so don't be late! Don't miss the excitement!"

Bruno and Cintia left the town square and raced each other down the street as the train pulled out of the station.

The sun came out, providing a little warmth amidst the gusts of cold winter air. The linden trees in the square had no leaves left on them, and the children's playground looked as lonely as the abandoned house itself.

The only store still open for business was Don Simón's bookshop. The store also loaned books and let anyone interested in reading the paper do so for free, though only after Don Simón was done with it himself, of course.

The smell of tomato sauce rose from the houses in Azul. The old women were preparing fresh spaghetti. At the inn, spaghetti with tomato sauce was also on the menu.

HIM

The train whistle became unbearable as the train left the station. Cintia, with one paper in her bicycle basket and another in her hand, parked her bike in front of her house. Bruno waited for her outside.

Although he was a close friend, Bruno did not go inside her house very often. Cintia's father didn't want his daughter to have friends. He was a solitary man with penetrating eyes. His presence made people uneasy. No one could contradict him, and it was no secret that he often got angry, especially with his daughter.

She greeted her father on the sidewalk.

"Cintia, don't stray far from the house," he said harshly. "As soon as María gets home from mass we'll sit down for lunch."

"But, I'm having lunch with Grandma! I promised I'd bring her the paper."

"I told you already, we are expecting you for lunch. Take her the paper and come right back. You know I don't like you hanging around outside in the middle of the day. And tell your grandmother not to expect you for lunch anymore," her father ordered.

But Cintia wasn't listening. She was already pedaling away, riding hard against the strong wind. Bruno followed without a word.

They were both very worried about the little house being for sale. A thousand ideas were going through their minds. That isolated refuge had been the scene of many of their meetings. They went there to read on the big rock, tell each other funny secrets and spy through the keyhole of the abandoned house.

On their way to Cintia's grandmother's, Bruno said, "I'll take you to your grandmother's house and then I'll go home for lunch. My mother's waiting for me."

Suddenly he slammed on the brakes with his right foot, leaving a furrow in the dirt. In a flash, he pulled out the slingshot that he kept in the back pocket of his pants, found a little rock on the road, put it in the holder and aimed.

Cintia watched without a word as a sparrow fell into the ditch right before her eyes. Bruno ran to fetch it and put it in his bicycle basket.

"Let's go!" he said.

As soon as Cintia was able to react, she cried, "You have no soul! You always ruin everything!"

And she left him standing there, as she always did when he behaved like that.

It was always the same with Bruno. When no one was watching, he would hunt for birds. Then he'd pluck them and give them to his mother to cook. She served them with cornmeal for dinner.

Cintia could not really love someone so merciless. What she did not know was that Bruno had used a slingshot instead of a BB gun, so she wouldn't be so shocked.

I don't understand girls, he thought as he headed home.

"I hate him! He's a murderer!" Cintia said to herself. "I don't know how he can do it, but he eats them, too!"

Sunday, noon. After a visit to the cemetery with Doña Hilda Ruverino, Grandmother Pina usually came home and prepared lunch. Then she would sit down next to the jasmine bush to wait for her granddaughter while she knit socks for the children of the orphanage.

She always found something useful to fill the time. She baked sweets and cakes to sell, she did laundry at the old folks' home, she mended pants for the children of the neighborhood, prepared liqueurs. All of this after doing her housework and tending to her vegetable garden.

Grandmother took a deep breath of the perfume from the jasmine bush. This was the fuel that kept her knitting needles going. And when the needles began to race, the memories flooded back. Cintia had heard them many times before – stories about the people who had come with her on the boat from Spain, and stories about the natives who had lived in the area of Azul long before that.

Pina kept on knitting, letting her memories unravel. She wanted to forget her daughter, Cintia's mother, who had dropped everything and left one day when Cintia was a small child. Pina had never forgiven her. She never found out why she had left, but even if she had, she felt that there was no reason that could justify leaving like that, abandoning a child as special as Cintia. She was angry at her daughter for what she had done.

She might not want to see her again, but she still missed her. She also wished she could understand Cintia's father. He was a heartless man who blamed the little girl for everything that had happened to him. Pina could not bear the fact that this man was the mayor's friend, that his shady business dealings and his love of gambling were the talk of the town.

A sudden noise shook her out of her dark thoughts.

"Who's there?"

The sound of a flower pot being knocked over told her it was Cintia. Then she heard Cintia muttering under her breath, blaming her bicycle for the overturned pot. She recognized the sound of the newspaper fluttering in the wind, followed by the sound of someone running after the paper. Then, another crash, as the little ceramic dwarf fell and broke into a thousand pieces.

This was the way Cintia usually arrived at her grandmother's house.

"Cintia, what's the matter?"she asked. "My little girl, I think you must have had an argument with Bruno."

Cintia didn't reply.

"I guess we all have to learn to live with our friends' flaws."

Cintia started crying.

"He must have killed a little bird."

Cintia cried harder.

"Come, tell me."

But Cintia just kept crying and crying.

She cried like she cried when her father's wife, María, forbade her to read at night. She cried as if a whole army of stepmothers had forbidden her to eat ice cream. She cried the way Cinderella cried when she couldn't go to the ball. Like Snow White when she was alone in the forest, afraid of the dark. Like

Hansel and Gretel when they were abandoned. Like the Ugly Duckling because he felt ugly. Like Alice, like…

She cried the way she cried when her father hit her, because whenever he was upset, which was often, he hit her.

BLUE SPAGHETTI

Grandmother Pina set her knitting aside. She dried Cintia's tears with a corner of her apron and went into the house with her.

"Look, I have a surprise for you. It was going to be a surprise for Bruno, too, but since you didn't come together he's going to have to miss it."

"Too bad for him."

The fire was going inside Grandmother's wood stove. She put a pot of water to boil on one of the burners. On the other burner she placed another pot with the tomato sauce she had prepared that morning. The aroma of onions, tomatoes and basil filled the air and penetrated the nooks and crannies of the house.

"It's not bird sauce, is it?"

"Cintia, how can you say such a thing? Come and sit down, and don't open your eyes until I tell you to."

When Cintia opened her eyes, she saw a huge dish of spaghetti, only this spaghetti was blue.

"Grandma, where did you get the spaghetti? Is it safe to eat?"

It was safe to eat, and they ate it all. They even dipped their bread in the sauce.

"Now will you tell me what's wrong?"

"I don't know what's wrong with me. I was just with Bruno. We went to the abandoned house, we saw some people near the house, we came back together... If only he wouldn't kill little birds... "

Cintia told her grandmother how she and Bruno had been talking away happily, making plans for later that afternoon, until they were cruelly interrupted by the tragic demise of that poor little bird.

"I hate him when he does that, Grandma. He's a murderer!"

"Yes, you're right, but what can you do?"

"Nothing! I know when he sees me he'll say that I'm being stupid. And I'm going to tell him that he's a murderer and that he deserves to be put behind bars."

"Aren't you exaggerating a little?"

The blue spaghetti was delicious and helped to chase away her sadness. Grandmother had also made mandarin orange juice, and an apple cake with lots of cream.

"You know, Cintia, people often behave in ways

we don't like and do things we'd rather they didn't do. Your grandfather was always doing things I didn't like."

"Did you get mad at him?"

"Yes, but I tried not to dwell on it."

"How?"

"I would talk to the pots and pans, the flowers. I even talked to the laundry! I shouted at everything, pretending I was shouting at Grandfather so that when he got back the next day, or the next night, all the bad feelings were gone."

"But that's impossible, Grandma. If I can't call Bruno a murderer to his face, looking him straight in the eye, nothing will change. The worst part is that he probably won't even care. I won't be his friend anymore. That's it, I'll never speak to him again."

Grandmother knew that in a day or two Cintia would get over her anger. In the meantime, she couldn't change her mind. That's how it is with tantrums. They take people by surprise, but they don't last long. Sometimes they go away with a few words. Other times only tears will drive the anger away.

"Grandma, are you going to tell me where you got the blue spaghetti?"

Grandmother Pina smiled, winked at her and began to clear the table. The dishes were left sparkling clean. The detergent removed the grease like magic. Now the kitchen smelled clean.

Cintia helped to dry the dishes. They left the glasses to dry upside down on the tea towel so they would stay shiny, without water stains.

"Will you stay with me for the *siesta*? Come on, don't think about the little birds. Bruno you can't forget, but the birds, yes."

"Only one thing can help me forget."

"What would that be, sweetheart?"

"Will you tell me the story about you and Grandfather?"

"Not again!"

"Please, Grandma. I'll tell you a story after, I promise."

"All right, let's go into the yard."

A long time ago, so long ago that I have trouble remembering, the hand of fate brought me to this town we call Azul. There were times when I felt emptiness in my chest, when sadness knocked at my door, but I kept smiling.

Your grandfather, Aníbal, came to Azul fleeing hunger, war and the barbarism and chaos Spain had plunged into. We were engaged at that time, and I stayed behind. He traveled by boat and later, he hid in a freight train. This is how he made his way to Azul. He did not choose this town. When they discovered him hiding in one of the wagons, they kicked him out of the train like a sack of wheat.

I've told you the story many times. My parents wouldn't let me travel unless I got married. But how could I marry when the groom was thousands of kilometers away?

In those days there was a special way to get married that saved me – marriage by proxy. We were married by a judge, even though there was an ocean between us.

And so I arrived here at the age of twenty-six. My husband was waiting for me in a little hut close to the brick works. The first thing we bought was a cow that we kept behind the house. We raised chickens, ducks and even a sheep.

Tending the vegetable garden was your grandfather's favorite pastime. He worked at the tannery, and in his free time he pruned bushes. The hut was small. We only had one room and a kitchen with a table and two benches.

And then there was the jasmine bush. I did my knitting sitting next to it. When it rained I sat close to the window that looked out on a dirt road. We also had an outhouse. In the beginning, I have to admit I was afraid to go to the bathroom. When I looked down, I could see the pit and I was afraid of falling in. But with time, I got used to it.

As the years passed, our life improved. We had good harvests of peaches, walnuts, apples and pears from our orchard. I learned to make and sell jams. Then, after a few years of living in this country, your mother was born. I used to get up early, light the fire, feed the chickens, milk the cow. Then I'd wake up your grandfather. He would drink a glass of rum or gin and leave for the tannery. When he came home he loved to find lunch ready. He always rushed through the meal so he could have a siesta before going back to work in the afternoon.

I would wake him up from his siesta with *mate* tea. He would sit in the garden to drink it, under the fig tree. He liked his *mate* strong and hot. I would go back and forth from the hut to the fig tree as many times as he needed to replenish the *mate*. If I left the kettle in the shade next to him, the water would get cold.

After he finished the tea, he would wash his face with the lukewarm water I poured into a washbasin for him. Then he would sit quietly, slowly waking up, until they blew the whistle at the sausage factory. This whistle told him it was time to go back to work at the tannery.

We liked being together and living like this. The birds would come to sing at our window. I would stay up until dawn sewing and blow out the candle before going to bed so he wouldn't wake up. I never asked him for money. With the money I earned from my small job, I had enough to pay for food.

He died of a heart attack when your mother was three, and after that I raised her on my own. Later on, I moved to this little house, bringing this jasmine bush with me as a reminder of those days. It was here in this house that your mother turned fifteen, here that she came back to feed you when you were a baby.

I got used to being alone and tried to keep myself in good spirits. I still keep wonderful memories of your grandfather in my heart, as well as a few other things – a leather suitcase, a pair of glasses and a pipe. I also have the photographs of your mother that you've seen a thousand times. She was a beautiful child. Almost as beautiful as you.

You know the rest of the story. I wish you could come to visit me more often and I wish your father would not get so angry at you. I wish we could find a way to be happy, live in peace and maybe, why not, even have another mayor. But my mother, your great-grandmother used to say, no evil lasts forever, and you'll see, my wishes will come true.

I think you know that my thoughts are always with a wonderful little girl, even when her life and the world around her put her in a bad mood. This girl is trying to find happiness, in spite of the fact that life hasn't been very generous to her.

I promise you, we will be happy together. We will build a world full of beautiful things out of our own stories and our imaginations. And whenever we feel sad we'll remember that we have one another, and then everything will be easier.

PUNISHMENT

"Grandma," said Cintia. "Why didn't you get married again after Grandfather died so many years ago?"

She didn't answer.

They finished cleaning up the kitchen and watering the plants. Grandmother put on her glasses to read the paper. The stories in the newspaper seemed like something from another planet.

"At least we find out about some things leafing through these pages, don't you think? It's good to find out about other cities, about what the president is saying."

"What president?"

"Our country's president, dear. He is our president, too. Even if he doesn't seem to know that we exist, he governs us. None of our presidents have ever visited Azul."

"Oh, Grandma, I remember what I wanted to tell you! The little blue house is up for sale!"

"No, Cintia. That house is not for sale."

"Yes, it is. There's a sign!"

"Cintia, I wish you wouldn't go there. Your father gets mad at me every time you do. He says that I put crazy ideas in your head. I don't have to tell you what your father will do to you if he finds out. You know he does nothing the mayor disapproves of. I don't want him sending you off to the nuns, where they'll only let you out on Sundays. We wouldn't be able to see each other, and we'd both suffer terribly."

"Bruno and I are going to find a way to get inside the house."

"You can't go into other people's houses just like that!"

"But the house doesn't belong to anyone. Although it has to belong to someone if it's got a FOR SALE sign on it."

"Look, Cintia, it's better not to get involved in things that are none of your business. Soon we'll all know who that house belongs to. But I can assure you it's not for sale."

As night fell, Cintia rode back home on her bicycle. She passed by Bruno's house and stood there for a while, but no one came out. She went to the corner and stood gazing at his house, but everything was very quiet. She continued on home and as soon as she got there, she locked herself in her room and began to read.

"Where are you, Cintia?" her father shouted. "Come here! I told you not to stay for lunch at your grandmother's house."

Cintia kept quiet. She knew that her father was like a tornado when he got mad. She knew not to say anything in situations where words could do nothing.

The books were soothing. She was reading *Jane Eyre*, which the bookseller, Don Simón, had lent her for the week. She loved it. She had already read it several times, crying each time. She held on to the book tightly and waited.

The door flew open, banging against the wall. This was how her father always entered her room.

"Ah, there you are!" he said, his face as red as a tomato.

"Yes."

"I told you not to stay for lunch at your grandmother's house, didn't I?"

"I'm sorry, Daddy."

"You know what happens when you don't do as I say. I told you already. If you keep going to see that old crone I'll send you to the school my friend Eduardo recommended, and you'll have to stay there until you're eighteen. Do you know what they do there to girls who don't behave? Do you want me to show you what happens to bad girls like you? You knew you were going to pay for disobeying me, didn't you?"

Yes, Cintia did know. Only too well. But she couldn't avoid it. Visiting with Grandmother was one of the nicest things in her life, and she wasn't about to give that up. She wasn't going to allow her father to forbid her from doing things, but sometimes she couldn't come up with anything to say.

And then what usually happened, happened again.

It was too ugly to tell, and Cintia could not talk about it because she was ashamed. Even though everyone knows everything that goes on in little towns, and even though what went on in her house was no secret, Cintia still believed that nobody else knew. It wasn't so strange that she thought this way, because no one took it upon themselves to help her, or so she felt. Fear and ignorance prevented outsiders from getting involved.

The next morning the larks came to wake Cintia up just as María, her stepmother, came into her room with her breakfast.

"Hi, María," said Cintia, as she touched her behind, trying to soothe the pain from her father's blows.

"You stayed up until God knows what time reading again. You don't understand, do you, Cintia? After all that's happened you still won't mend your ways, child. And you know that after you, I get it, too. Now your father has asked me to keep an eye on the candles. You're using too many candles each week. Look, the new one I left for you last night is gone. This is too much, Cintia! Child, please don't make your father angry. You have to try to be like me. Just do everything you can to please him."

Cintia rarely started the day in a good mood, and it took her until lunchtime to wake up completely. At school she often felt like she wasn't really there. This morning her legs hurt. María had to struggle to get her out of bed.

Cintia was tired of María's suggestions, could not understand why she stayed and subjected herself to her father's mistreatment. She was the one who was free to leave if she wanted to! As she observed her father's wife, Cintia began to understand, just a little, why her own mother had left.

María did not seem too concerned, though.

"Up, get up! I want to listen to the bad news," she shouted.

Fortunately there was little if any crime in Azul. Everyone had known each other forever. So bad news usually came from somewhere else, and María enjoyed listening to it on the radio.

"It's Monday, Cintia. Get up. You can't be late for school. Come on!"

"María, please let me skip school. Let me sleep in a bit."

"It's your father's orders. You know him. God forbid that I let you skip classes. I'll end up hanging from a rope at the police station, tortured by the mayor."

Grumbling and muttering, Cintia got up, tidied her room, got dressed and left for school.

She knew she would see Bruno, and that by now the whole school would know about their argument. That's what she hated most about the town – the way everyone learned about everything almost before it happened. She often wondered what the townspeople said about her father, but that gossip didn't reach her.

No one would tell a daughter bad things about her father.

It was often difficult for Cintia to get through Monday mornings. Sometimes she felt so alone. Arguing with Bruno was like being inside an empty room with no light and nothing to do. Could Grandmother be right? Was it so important to try to understand people?

No! She didn't want to understand Bruno. She couldn't understand how he could kill little birds and then eat them. She could not bring herself to understand someone who could kill defenseless beings.

Take the morning as it came – that was all she could do.

HIM AGAIN

Bruno was the handsomest boy in grade seven. He was thin and you could see all his ribs, but he was cute. He was always chewing fruit-flavored gum, and he wore a cap over his lanky hair. During recess he played with the other boys, shooting at birds with slingshots. They weren't supposed to bring slingshots to school, but they were easy to hide.

All the girls were crazy about Bruno, but he didn't pay attention to them. He only came over to the girls' yard if he had something to tell Cintia, and she would give him a lollipop or a bacon sandwich.

If a teacher saw them talking, they would be sent to the office. The schoolyard was split in two by a line the third-grade teacher had drawn in chalk. The boys played to the left of the line, the girls to the right. There was no running. Running was one of the nicest things to do during recess, but it wasn't allowed.

But the boys didn't pay attention to this rule, and they ran around the yard anyway. Sometimes they pulled at each other's jackets and the buttons would fall off. The buttons were always missing from Bruno's jackets.

The teachers said that the chalk line between the girls' and the boys' side of the yard had no special reason for being there. The third-grade teacher just said that the boys were rougher and the girls were more delicate. Bruno crossed the line and this charmed Cintia to no end. But as soon as she saw a dead bird, the charm evaporated, and all she felt was confusion. Bruno's friends were a lot worse than he was. They not only killed birds, they also murdered hares and ducks. Sometimes Bruno went hunting with them, and he would come back with a box full of animals. Afterwards, they would eat dove cutlets, pickled hare and duck *à l'orange*.

Mondays had always been tragic for Cintia, but this one was more so. Bruno was not at school. Even though they'd had a serious argument, Cintia would still have enjoyed watching Bruno from a distance. She didn't even want to go to school if Bruno wasn't there.

And as if that weren't enough, she had finished reading *Jane Eyre*. Every time she finished reading a book, she felt a void that only reading another book could fill. The problem was, she couldn't always get another one to replace it fast enough. Besides, she only became immersed in a new story after she started the book a few times.

She had been thinking a lot about the abandoned house and knew that if it was sold, there would be nowhere to go with Bruno – if they ever made up, of course.

Nothing made sense to her without her friend. She realized that she was unhappy when he wasn't there, and she sank into a sadness as foggy and dark as the worst winter morning of her life.

For a while now Cintia had felt as though her heart were leaping out of her chest every time she saw Bruno. She said foolish things in his presence, was unable to control herself. She thought about him from morning until night and went to sleep with images of him in her head. His face appeared to her when she was doing the horrible math homework her teacher gave her and when she was in science class. She thought about him and hated him at the same time. She couldn't make sense of her feelings.

The bell finally rang, marking the end of the horrible school day.

Cintia was supposed to go straight home, but she had a problem. She absolutely had to go by Don Simón's bookshop to get a new book. She could not do without a story to read under these circumstances.

She had to find another book so she could identify with the character and compare her own sadness to that of the heroine. Or just cry, like when Beth died in *Little Women*. She read that part of the book over and over until the tears welled up. Once she started to cry over Beth's death, more tears – the tears Cintia did not normally cry for herself – flowed out, too. Though she was young, Cintia had lots of tears stored inside because of the things she had to go through.

She decided to ask Don Simón for an adult book. She was ready to read a big drama.

DON SIMÓN

Don Simón's bookshop was next to the station. He sold books, new and old, had magazines for exchange and a file of all the Sunday papers going back many years so the public could consult them. In the same shop there was a case full of erasers, pencils, paint and notebooks. He was the only person in town who sold school supplies.

Even so, people didn't buy a lot. Sales were few and far between, to the point that, in order to keep the business going, Don Simón had to reduce the size of the store, with all the inconveniences this implied. It took him a long time to make his decision, but there was no other way. People didn't buy books any more, so he decided he would lend them out, like at a library. He still had to pay taxes, however, so to cover his costs, he rented out the front of the bookstore.

Clarita was the first person who approached him when she saw the FOR RENT sign. She was a very popular lady who ran a sewing supplies business out of her home. Clarita was Azul's living newspaper. She knew about the lives of everyone who came into her shop, and even some who didn't.

When she learned that Don Simón was renting out the front of the bookshop, she said she could use it. Don Simón accepted her offer but asked that she sell only needles, thread and buttons.

In the beginning she honored the agreement and moved just a few things into the old bookshop. Soon, however, she began adding a bit of yarn here, some fabric there, so that by the time the bookseller finally took notice, the section that would have been best suited for displaying literary classics was suddenly filled with toys, shoes and even second-hand furniture. Fortunately, his renter never crossed the dividing line – which no longer existed – between the sewing supplies store and the section he devoted to books.

Don Simón was happy to stay at the back because this way people who came to shop in Clarita's store did not bother him. To tell the truth, more people came into her store than his, even when he wasn't lending the books instead of selling them.

"People need a little fabric or thread more than

they need books," Clarita said, trying to convince him to rent her the whole store. "You should retire and give up the business, my friend, so you can live without worries."

The old women who went to the store in the mornings to buy elastic or a piece of ribbon for the baby stayed around for a while drinking *mate* with the shopkeeper. None of them quite understood why Don Simón was so stubborn about going on with his bookstore. As for the bookseller, he turned on the radio so he wouldn't have to listen to their chatter.

Cintia, on the other hand, understood her beloved bookseller very well. She knew it wasn't easy to let go of what one loved most in life.

"Clarita, you could display your merchandise better if you had more space," said one of her customers.

"I really don't understand why he wants to go on with the store at his age," Clarita replied. "He doesn't even sell the books! He's always had these ideas about sharing everything. God knows where he gets them from. I guess he figured reading would somehow pay off in the long run."

"Ah, and then he complains that his eyesight is failing. Of course, all he does is read all day…"

And so Don Simón became part of the gossip, just like the stories people listened to on the local radio station at nine in the evening.

After school that tragic Monday, Cintia rode her

bike to the bookstore. She rode standing on the ped-als because her bottom hurt so much. She opened the door, heard the little bells and noticed how all the old women turned to look at her at the same time.

Because she had been so well brought up, she greeted everyone with a nod before she went to look for her friend at the back of the store. She crossed the wooden floor, which bounced at every step, causing the furniture to shift a little. The smell of the sewing supplies store mixed with the smell of the bookstore. The clacking old women followed her with their eyes.

When she got to the wooden counter, Don Simón took the pipe out of his mouth and asked, "Have you finished the book already?"

Clarita whispered something that Cintia didn't hear or didn't want to hear.

"Yes, I finished it, Don Simón."

"Well, I'll give you another one."

"I want one that will make me cry a lot."

"Do you want one about youths, as you like to call them?"

"No, this time I want one about grownups. The kind that parents don't want their children to read. And I want a book set in my favorite period, when women wore long dresses and wrote with quill pens. You know, when there was no electricity."

"Let me see what I can find."

Don Simón was used to people in the store talking about him behind his back and he tried to ignore the gossip. Cintia wasn't used to it, however, and it really bothered her to hear the things the women were saying.

"Look how he's perverting the mind of that girl."

"A girl should not be reading things like that."

It made her angry, but Cintia couldn't say anything, because Clarita was Bruno's grandmother.

"What about your friend?" asked the bookseller, without looking at her.

"I don't know…"

"What do you mean you don't know? Hmmm."

Cintia looked in Clarita's direction and came closer to Don Simón.

"I can't talk right now," she said, "but if you come to the square this afternoon, I'll tell you everything. I'm having a bad day. On top of everything, the little blue house is for sale. Did you hear about it? So, yes, I'm in a bad mood."

"Really? Don't worry. The little blue house is not for sale."

"Yes, it is! There's a FOR SALE sign on it."

Don Simón started smoking his pipe again. After holding the pipe between his lips for a while, he walked over to the shelves and handed her another book.

"I don't know if this will make you cry, but I'm sure you'll like it."

"*Wuthering Heights.*"

"The author is the sister of the woman who wrote *Jane Eyre*." The bookseller smiled.

"Then for sure I'm going to love it." And Cintia left with *Wuthering Heights* under her arm.

The old women couldn't have guessed what Cintia was taking with her, because they knew nothing about books.

"Poor girl. Someone will have to tell her family that this old fellow is ruining her mind. But who cares about this girl? With a father and mother like hers..."

"Don't meddle," said Clarita. "Her grandmother tries to protect her. As much as she can, anyway. The girl was born that way, poor thing!"

DISAPPOINTMENT

Don Simón arrived at the square just after three o'clock. He sat under the linden trees and began to read. Cintia arrived with her book, too.

"What's the matter with this girl?" Don Simón wondered out loud, without raising his eyes from his book.

"It's Bruno. We had an argument."

"Ah, but that won't last long."

"No, this time I won't talk to him ever again. He killed a little bird right in front of my eyes."

Don Simón listened without looking up, and kept on reading.

"How do you stop being a killer?" Cintia asked.

"It's not easy."

"That's what I think. What are you reading?" she asked, touching the cover of the book.

"I'm reading *The Metamorphosis*. It's the story of a man who turns into an insect."

"That's what should happen to Bruno. Does it say how you do it?"

"No, it just happens. The man in the story didn't set out to become a bug."

"Oh, too bad! I'm also worried that the little abandoned house is up for sale."

"I told you, the house is not for sale."

"But the sign says it is."

At that moment Don José arrived with a thermos of *mate*, and Don Simón couldn't go on reading, let alone talk about the abandoned house.

Cintia took her bicycle and rode to the little house. She did it without thinking, without looking back. She had put her book in her bicycle basket.

Everything was very quiet as she approached the pond. Bruno's bicycle was very close to the weeping willows. She hurried toward him, not saying hello, trying to seem indifferent.

"Hi," he said.

"Hi," she answered, but only to be polite. Then she asked, "Are you going in?"

"No, Cintia, I can't right now. I have to get back."

"You didn't go to school."

"I've been busy."

"Are you mad at me?"

"Of course not."

"And you're leaving without saying anything else? You seem strange…" Cintia kept looking at him.

He put together his slingshot. Then he got on his bike and left.

She followed him at a safe distance so he wouldn't feel that he was being followed. She saw him go into Julián's house.

Cintia went home in a worse mood than ever. This was how it always happened. She would promise herself that she wouldn't talk to him, but she ended up doing it just the same.

When she got home she told María.

"Do you see?"

"Men are all the same," María said as she cleaned the window panes.

"I know. That's why I'm never going to get married."

"Are you going to the dance?"

"What dance?"

"The winter break dance. They're going to pick four princesses to represent us at the Jacaranda Festival."

"Oh, that's a long time away. I don't know whether I'm going. I don't want to be one of those poor girls who apply to be princesses. Being a princess is not that nice."

"Bruno's going and so is his mother."

One of the problems with María was that she knew everything that went on in Azul, mostly because she worked as a cleaning lady in many people's homes. On top of that, she couldn't keep anything she overheard to herself.

Cintia wasn't surprised to find out that her friend would be going, because everybody went to the town dances. So she paid no attention to María and went off to read.

Soon Soledad arrived.

"Want to know who asked me to the dance?"

"No," said Cintia.

"Julián."

"That's great!"

"And you?"

Cintia didn't say anything. Nobody had invited her, but she didn't care. These things never mattered much to her.

"You know what?" Soledad went on, "Julián told me that Bruno is going with Belén, one of his cousins from the city who's here with her family till the end of the holidays."

Cintia said nothing, but she felt her heart sink like a rock. Rage rose up in her throat, and her mouth became as dry as a desert.

"You should see how nice Belén is. They already let her wear makeup because, well, you know city girls. You should have seen the way Pedro was staring at her."

Pedro was Bruno's friend and the biggest slob in the world. He went around with his shoelaces undone, dirty face, dirty nails, and even though he was in seventh grade, he couldn't read or spell.

"No, I don't know. What are they like?" said Cintia, struggling with tears that were welling up without warning.

"Well, they are more modern. All the boys are in love with her. She arrived yesterday on the 11:30 train and she wears blue nail polish. She has a streak of red hair in her bangs and apparently she also likes to hunt for little birds…"

Soledad left, leaving Cintia, her mouth agape, wanting to scream.

She took refuge in the book Don Simón had given her.

ANGER

It was almost nighttime. Grandmother wasn't knitting next to the jasmine bush because the winter cold had forced her into the kitchen. Even so, she heard the bicycle crashing and the flower pots being knocked over.

"I know," Grandmother Pina said. "You had an argument with your friend again."

"He's stupid," Cintia replied "He's an idiot!"

"What happened?"

With worry gnawing at her stomach, Cintia told her, in a confused fashion, everything that had happened since they had last seen each other.

"If I had him in front of me I'd tear his hair out, I'd punch a hole in his bicycle tires, break his slingshot..." she sobbed, heartbroken.

Grandmother waited. She made Cintia a banana shake. After just a few minutes, the tears were flowing less abundantly down Cintia's cheeks.

"And Bruno invited a foreigner to the dance at the club!"

Grandmother did not answer.

"They say she likes to hunt little birds and she's from the city. She wears makeup and everything."

"Men are in such a rush," said Grandmother. "They let themselves be seduced by the first flirt that comes along."

"What am I going to do?"

"Go to the dance," answered Grandmother.

"With who?"

"We'll see. First you have to find out whether what you heard is true. And if it is, you'll have to look your best and not let your anger show. How did you find out about this? Did Bruno tell you?"

"No."

"Then, my child, go and find out. One shouldn't believe everything one hears."

"Why shouldn't I believe it, Grandma, when he's capable of killing little birds? María is right. Men are all the same."

Grandmother was very sad to hear the things Cintia was saying.

"Go home, Cintia. It's late already. Go to bed and listen to the story on the radio."

By nine that night everyone was sitting up, their radios on, ready to listen to the voice telling the familiar tale that had so much to do with the history of Azul.

LEGEND 2

A man and his family were fleeing from other men, who were both like them but different at the same time. They were similar because they were men. Different because they were white. They believed they had the right to kill other men.

The people they were hunting came upon this land after a night of endless walking. They had crossed huge expanses of land. They set up their shacks close to an ombú tree, the only tree for hundreds of kilometers around. Settling close to fifteen other fleeing families, all mourning their lost brothers and sisters, they began a new life.

Close to their camp was a pond that they named Capybara, after the animals that had greeted them when they arrived. The lilies were blooming, and the pink reeds sheltered all kinds of birds that came to feed on the flowers.

None of the new arrivals knew how long the peace

would last. Each dawn brought the promise of another day and, with it, the fear that they would be driven out of the land again and killed.

Time passed, but luck was not on the side of the natives. Yellow fever soon killed most of them. Only Ailín and her mother and two or three other families survived the plague. The settlement was no longer a camp. It was reduced to being a group of wanderers without a home. Fearing death, the survivors burned their huts and built new ones.

They had to begin anew.

Months later, new rails were laid a few kilometers away, and a new train station was built. Progress was calling at their door, and the settlement moved closer to the station.

With the train came men who weren't concerned by the presence of a few native dwellers. They also came from faraway lands, and they were fleeing other plagues. Slowly, the sad little settlement became a tiny village, with houses built precariously out of mud and straw by people from many different places.

And once again, there was a new beginning.

Ailín the native orphan girl lamented that her father had not lived to see these changes. Some things come about when it's too late. The pain of losing him did not lessen with this new life. She had lost her way of life, her way of being in the world. She was part of a tribe no longer. Now they were merely a part of a small village.

INVITATION

Everything reminded Cintia of Bruno. She read and reread the lyrics of songs he had sent her in the third grade, looked at the little drawings he had made for her even before he knew how to write. A thousand thoughts played themselves out in her head, but not one of them gave her insight into the behavior of the one person who had always been her friend.

She read *Wuthering Heights* and saw herself in Catherine Earnshaw. Catherine had a stern father who did not tolerate boys as friends, just like Cintia's father. Heathcliff, Cathy's friend, reminded her of Bruno.

In literature you could always find people who had suffered like you.

I know we've always argued. That's not new. But before we both always wanted to go into the little house, Cintia thought, heartbroken.

The next morning she woke up with a fever. As usual, the first person who came to see her was her grandmother Pina, who came without her father's knowledge. Grandmother knew to visit when Cintia was alone in the house. She walked slowly, arriving at Cintia's house looking as if she had traveled for miles. She rubbed Cintia's chest and gave her a strawberry-flavored medicine.

Later, Pedro unexpectedly knocked at her door and invited her to the dance. She wasn't ready to give him an answer. He had never visited her before.

"So?" Pedro asked.

"Under one condition."

"What would that be?"

"That you don't tease me for being thin, that you don't throw pieces of chalk at my head, that you don't talk to me with your mouth full, that you don't breathe all over me when you are sweaty and, above all, that you swear under oath that after this dance you will never invite me to a dance ever again, for the rest of your life. And another thing. Don't come to my house covered in mud. And clean your nails."

"It's a deal," said Pedro. And he left, leaving a trail of mud in Cintia's room.

Why is he so clumsy? she wondered.

Outside, the birds were chirping happily, and people were busy talking about the upcoming dance, about what they would wear. The women were already sewing their gowns. At the club they had put a fresh coat of paint on the metal chairs and tables. The townspeople painted the borders of the sidewalks and the trunks of the linden trees with lime. The old women swept the streets. Don Darwin, the club caretaker, was getting ready to make the spicy pork sausage sandwiches he would have for sale, while his wife prepared the large punch bowls she would fill with orange juice.

The upcoming dance made Cintia think of the difficult times ahead. She had no choice, however, but to accept the situation as it was. She was used to the fact that things rarely went as she wished. She needed a mother and didn't have one. She wished she had a kind father instead of one who was violent and angry. She wished she had a grandfather.

Luckily, once she lost herself in a book, she forgot about the difficulties of her life.

She kept reading *Wuthering Heights*. Mr. Earnshaw told Catherine she should pray to God and ask for forgiveness. Cintia's father kept telling her that some day she would have to pay for everything she had eaten. Cathy's father confessed to her that he could not love her. How could a father say that to his daughter, Cintia wondered. Catherine and Heathcliff's moor was like the little blue house for Cintia and Bruno.

She had to keep reading. The candles burned

while the wind outside pounded at the window panes. Cintia didn't make a sound so her father would not find out her secret, that she read during the night until she could no longer make out the words.

Cintia couldn't understand why her father hated her to read. She also couldn't understand why he punished her so. He was always angry – not just at her, but at everyone. He was a man who could barely laugh. He did not treat María very well and never wanted to see Grandmother. He only got along with the mayor because they had known each other since they were children. As some people said, "God makes them, and they stick together."

Grandmother had told her a thousand times that it was useless to try to understand her father's anger. Better to say nothing when he said ugly things, no matter how hard it was. By staying silent, Cintia would avoid having worse things happen to her. Grandmother often told her granddaughter to hold on until she could come up with something that might help them both in the long run. She didn't realize that Cintia kept quiet, not just because her grandmother told her to, but because she got scared when her father lost his temper.

Grandmother was always quite mysterious and rarely said things clearly. Yet, because she had told her to hold on and accept it, Cintia tried. Before she left the house that day, Grandmother reminded Cintia again not to tell her father that she had come to take care of her.

ONE WEEK LATER

A week passed. Cintia was anxious for Bruno to know that she was going to the dance with Pedro. Even though the chances were slim, she kept hoping that Bruno would regret having invited Julián's cousin, especially once he found out that she would be going with Pedro.

"Will you help me, Cintia?" María asked while she set the table for lunch.

"I can't today. I have to go for a fitting for the dress I'm wearing to the dance."

"But you've never cared about clothes before," said María. "Are you going with someone?"

"Yes," said Cintia, thinking that this would be the perfect time to tell her who she was going with. María would quickly tell everyone who cared to listen. "I'm going with Pedro."

"The one with the muddy shoes?"

Cintia was still getting over her cold.

Grandmother came to visit her at siesta time to make sure her granddaughter got some rest. She took advantage again of Cintia's father's absence and gave her some extra chest rubs to make her cough go away. She read her stories from *One Thousand and One Nights*.

Grandmother was so good at reading from books without pictures. Cintia preferred to listen to a story without looking at the illustrations, so that way that she could imagine the characters in her own way. The pictures in books never looked like the ones she created in her mind, and she was always disappointed. That's what had happened with *Jane Eyre*. She could never tell who the people on the cover were. Was it Miss Temple, or was it Jane as a grown-up? The expression in the eyes of the two women on the cover were so similar, they could be mother and daughter, Cintia thought. But Jane was an orphan. And even if that were her mother, Cintia would have imagined her differently.

Grandmother had suggested she read *Tom Sawyer*, but she had already read it. She liked the part where Tom kissed Becky the best. What if she got sick like Becky? Would Bruno be as desperate as Tom?

The kids in the novel were imaginary, but Bruno was as real as she was. When Tom was overcome with worry, he wanted to die, at least for a few days.

And after they gave him up for dead he realized that he loved Becky. What if she played dead?

No, she thought, better not. When she came back to life, her father would kill her for sure, and that would be worse.

Two Sundays had passed since her argument with Bruno. She didn't know how to find out whether he had visited the little blue house. In town, rumors came and went about the house being for sale. The mayor's wife took some tourists to look at the place. Visits became more frequent because more people from other towns were coming to see the house, though just from the outside. After so many years of neglect, people were more intrigued than ever, trying to figure out who the owner was.

If the visitors wanted to see the pond, they had to pay an extra peso. They could take home a souvenir, but at a price. Leaves, grass, slivers, jacaranda flowers and dried forget-me-nots were available for sale. They were even selling a handwritten history of the house.

The tours were such a success that the mayor was thinking of adding extra tours during the week. The most curious came by car, motorcycle, horse-drawn buggy and truck.

To please his friend, the mayor, Cintia's father had again forbidden her to visit the house. But she went anyway.

What she wanted was to be all alone on a desert island. She didn't want to hear from anyone. She just wanted to be by herself. And she wanted Bruno to miss her. She wanted to die like Tom Sawyer for a few days and find out that Bruno could not live without her.

Instead, she decided to go on reading and forget about the things that came pouring out of her head like waterfalls.

ENTANGLEMENT

Saturday morning. Bruno fell into the trap just as Cintia had planned. As if that weren't enough, he set out angrily for Grandmother Pina's house. He arrived the same way Cintia always did, finishing off whatever his friend had managed to leave half-broken the last time she had fallen off her bicycle.

"Bruno, is that the way to come into someone's house?"

"Is Cintia here?"

Grandmother replied that she wasn't.

He told her he was furious because he had found out that Pedro was taking her to the dance.

"And who were you going to go with?"

"With Cintia. I even argued with Julián because he wanted to dump his cousin on me."

"So, why didn't you invite her?"

"I was waiting for the right time. The fact is, she

was mad at me. You know how she gets when she's upset about something. But now I'm going to have to invite that show-off cousin of Julián's just to make her really mad!" he said, and then he left.

The town was abuzz with the dance. Everyone was hoping the little abandoned house that turned blue in November wouldn't sell before the dance. Who would buy it? They knew so much and so little about that house. In Azul, as in all small towns, no two people had the same version of the facts.

For Bruno and Cintia, the confusion about who would go with whom to the dance kept growing. Grandmother Pina could not figure out how to make things better. The town was riddled with arguments, prejudices, shameful thoughts and opinions that were voiced and misunderstood.

"This is what happens when people get carried away with gossip," Grandmother thought.

What would happen if things never got sorted out? So many people never make up because of idle talk.

She thought about the story that had been broadcast on the radio the night before.

LEGEND 3

The railroad kept expanding, and the station and the village kept growing. People came and settled. Ailín had started to enjoy the pond. She would gather reeds in the spring and help her mother work the loom.

After a while the people built a square in the middle of the village. Linden trees grew there along with plants from the seeds settlers had brought with them in their suitcases. Soon the government sent its representatives to the station – a delegate and a priest.

Among the people who had come from Spain was Don Manuel Iraola. He was thirty-nine years old when he arrived in the village with his nineteen-year-old son Joaquín. A man with much money, he bought land close to the pond because he was drawn by the trees that grew on the shore. He immediately hired people to build a kiln and make bricks, and he began to *build what soon became the most beautiful house in the area. He had it painted white.*

Ailín and her mother lived in a hut very close to the white house. Soon Don Manuel hired the girl to work in the big house. Her mother didn't want her to work for a white man, but she had no choice. No one was buying the blankets she made on her loom, and they could not go on living in abject poverty. For thirteen years they had been living in the place she and Aloe had chosen the night they fled from the white men. Some bad feelings were impossible to get rid of and, even though the world around them had changed, none of the survivors of the Indian camp could ever forget how they had been persecuted.

By now Ailín had lived longer among the whites than among her own people. She could recognize goodness in others, and she saw that Don Manuel Iraola was a good white man. He was a writer, and he loved to read by the pond. He drank mate *from a gourd and let Ailín into all parts of the house.*

She had never seen brick floors, or so much furniture. The kitchen in his house was larger than Ailín's whole hut. Three rooms were built around the main sitting room, the dining room and the bathroom. This was the first house in the village with a bathroom built inside, and a water closet. Before that, people had used outhouses.

Without intending to, Don Manuel became like a

father to the native girl. In the beginning Ailín could not get used to so much comfort, and she wandered around the rooms gazing at the beds, the like of which she had never seen, much less slept in.

Before she died, her mother asked Ailín to swear that she would never trust white people. The day the native girl was left without a mother, Don Manuel asked her to come and live with him and his son in their house. He taught her manners, how to eat, how to write, though she did not want to learn.

She did not want to stop using the blankets she wore around her body, did not want to wear dresses. She could not erase from her heart the seeds planted there by her father and mother. She was mistrustful and afraid of white people. Her braids remained as black as they had always been and she continued to go barefoot. She knew how to weave cloth on a loom, so she wove curtains and ponchos for Don Manuel, which he wore proudly. She prepared the best locros. She went into Don Manuel's fields to look for corn, which she soaked overnight. She picked squash, onions and chilis from his vegetable garden. She made stews of turkey and beef, saved chicken feet for the broth and made mazamorra.

Every day, she got up at dawn, before the cock crowed. She lit the fire in the kitchen wood stove, boiled water and prepared mate for Don Manuel. Then she spent two or three hours grinding corn.

Ailín and Joaquín became friends, but she never forgot the promise she had made to her mother. Don Manuel would ask Ailín to tell them stories, and both father and son listened with interest and consternation to the tales of Ailín's sad past. She felt very comfortable with them.

Joaquín found out many things about Ailín. He taught her to read and write and then told her his story – that of an immigrant. He told her about the sea, and together they wrote letters, poems and recipes.

Joaquín would ask, "Let's see, how do you make pickled hare? Please, write it down."

She would write, Laurel leaves, broth and lard.

"Ah, but I want to know how it is prepared, not just the ingredients."

So she would write, Place the hare under briskly running water until it turns white...

"Very good."

And so the pleasure of writing grew in her.

Then came the poems.

Ailín ended up writing for hours at a time, sitting by the edge of the pond.

Joaquín left letters for her on the bench. She took them with her and read them while she peeled potatoes. Then she read and reread them until she knew them by heart.

BLOWS

Saturday, after lunch. Cintia was lying down in her room, waiting for Bruno to show some sign of life. She wanted him to know how angry she was that he was taking another girl to the dance.

The rumbling of the trucks passing through town filled her room. As soon as they were gone, however, the air cleared, as if they had never existed. There was a strong wind. María put the chickens in the coop so they wouldn't freeze to death.

"Cintia!" her father shouted, "Cintia, get over here!"

Cintia knew instantly that her father was angry again, but it was going to be difficult to figure out what was bothering him. Her father's tempers came suddenly and without explanation.

What have I done now? she thought as she left her room.

"I told you I don't want you spending the whole day reading. There's plenty of work to be done. If you don't have enough to do, go to the factory and ask Don Cholo for a job."

"But…"

"Did you go to the little blue house?"

"I…"

"Cintia, tell me, have you been to the little blue house? Yes or no?"

"Who told you?"

"Everyone knows everything around here," her father said angrily. "If it's true, or if something else is going on, you'd better start running right now. I'm not about to pay any fines because of you! You made me look bad in front of the mayor, you little devil." He raised his hand and grabbed Cintia by her braids. He dragged her into the kitchen and, teeth clenched, he uttered the words Cintia was so sick of hearing.

"You and that filthy boy went to the abandoned house again. I've told you a thousand times not to go there! You have a devil inside you."

"Bruno is not a filthy boy. He's my friend!" cried Cintia. She knew that her father would punish her for saying that.

"Don't contradict me."

"I'm not –"

And what always happened, happened again.

Her father beat her.

He screamed at her, his teeth clenched and his screams loud. Cintia clenched her teeth, too, and thought about her mother. She thought about Catherine Earnshaw, how her father was mean to her, too. And she remembered that on the day of her death, as Mr. Earnshaw stroked his daughter's head, Catherine had asked him why he hadn't tried to be a better person.

There were things Cintia would never be able to say to her father.

Cintia kept her tears to herself. Her father had turned into an animal, his large hands causing terrible pain. His words were just as painful.

Cintia was punished, and her punishments were always the same. Her father forbade her to do the things she liked the most. She was not allowed to see her grandmother, even though she hadn't been to the house for weeks.

He deprived her of seeing the people she truly cared for – Bruno and Grandmother Pina.

"María, ask him to forgive me," said Cintia as soon as she could talk. But María did not dare say anything to Cintia's father out of fear that he might hit her, too.

"Don't worry, Cintia. We'll figure out something."

María was a good person, but she would never

dare confront the man who had chosen her for his partner. She was very poor, and one of the reasons she had agreed to be his wife was that he offered her a decent house to live in. She had imagined that married life would be hard, but never this hard. Like many women, she believed that the man she lived with would change. But, with every passing day, he just got worse.

It had been hard for him to get over the humiliation of Cintia's mother leaving him. His life was not simple. It isn't easy to live in a town where you are being watched and talked about all the time. Of course, this was no justification for his violent temper. People never know quite what to do in circumstances like these, when a father beats his child. The townspeople preferred to think that it would go away, that things would fall into place at some point. So no one got involved.

Cintia needed her grandmother more and more. And today more than ever.

She picked up *Wuthering Heights* and kept reading. When she couldn't see the letters anymore she dried her tears with a handkerchief. She wanted to die from grief, like Cathy. She wanted Bruno to be like Heathcliff. She wanted her father to be good. She wanted her mother to come home. She wanted her grandmother to take her away from this hell.

THE LONG WAIT

Grandmother came. Nobody opened the door so she started to shout, standing outside the house that had once been her daughter's.

Her son-in-law came out. "Go away," he said. "Cintia doesn't want to see you!"

"You're lying. I won't leave until I talk to her."

"Then you'll have to take a seat and wait. And if you keep bothering me, I won't let you see her ever again."

"I'm tired of your threats! I won't leave until you let me see my granddaughter."

Grandmother sat down in the wooden armchair and waited.

Cintia was still reading *Wuthering Heights*. She had almost finished it for the second time. She was a fast reader. She kept thinking of going away to a desert island, or maybe forcing the lock to the abandoned house and hiding out there.

Grandmother did not move from the wooden armchair, but Cintia's father stayed home to make sure she did not come in.

"He'll have to go out at some point," Pina thought. "On Saturdays Juan goes out drinking with his buddies at the club."

Saturday was coming to an end. María kept bringing Grandmother Pina her *mate*. Grandmother looked into the distance, her gaze lost on the horizon and beyond. She thought back to her childhood, her parents, her family life in that place so far away that she had never gone back. She thought about the suffering everyone must go through for their loved ones, how painful some choices can be.

She had chosen to stay in this town, but she missed her childhood home. She had made up her mind never to go back, so that the memories of those long-ago days would remain intact.

She remembered everything so clearly. Those familiar faces were so fresh in her mind, she wondered if time were playing tricks on her. Maybe it hadn't been so long since she had left her country after all.

She realized she would have to move quickly with her plan to help Cintia. Someone from the city would surely be able to help her. She could not just sit by as this man mistreated her dear little girl.

She had to be careful, wait for just the right

moment to report him. Things would fall into place, she thought, but she had to be careful, because a girl abandoned by her mother and mistreated by her violent father could end up living in a reformatory. If she didn't succeed, things could get even worse. Juan would not think twice about having Cintia committed to an institution.

"What are you still doing here?"

"I must see my granddaughter."

"And I have to go out."

"Then let me come in. Why do you take away the things Cintia cherishes so much?"

Juan scratched his head. María dried her hands on her apron. She looked at Grandmother and said,

"It's late, Pina. Why don't you go home?"

"I'll stay here until morning if I have to. That way the whole town will know that you're not letting me see my own granddaughter, if they don't know already."

Juan glared at her. He didn't seem as angry now. Opening the screen door, he said, "Come in, but be careful, I'll be listening to everything you tell her. Don't forget, I can have you chased out of town if I want."

NEWS

Grandmother Pina got up very stiffly from the armchair. She had been sitting for too long, waiting to see her grandchild. Cintia's father took over the chair she had vacated.

"Cintia, child," said Grandmother. "It would be better if you didn't go to the little blue house again. María told me all about it."

"He's bad, Grandma, he's bad!"

"He's your father. You have to do as he says."

Grandmother knew that Juan was listening, so she had to be clever with the way she carried out her plan. "Besides, I have news," she whispered into Cintia's ear. "Yesterday afternoon the buyer of the little blue house was here…"

"It can't be."

"Yes, it can. You were right. They say the mayor even took the person inside the house. Some people are saying the little blue house will be torn down to make room for a milk-bottling plant. Others think they'll just turn it into farm land. But I'm sure that in the end it won't sell. I promise you."

"Then it's true?" Cintia said anxiously. "But you won't let them sell it, will you, Grandma?"

"Well…"

Pina had to watch what she said and made a sign so Cintia wouldn't ask any more questions. They continued talking in whispers.

"But can they sell something that doesn't belong to anyone?"

"Two black cars drove right through town down the dirt road to the house. The mayor was in one of them. We shouldn't get involved. I smell trouble."

Cintia didn't say anything.

"The people who saw them said they stayed in the house for five minutes and left," she said in a whisper, and then she raised her voice. "You have to do as your father says," she said, with a wink.

Cintia listened to her grandmother. A little while later she fell asleep, and her grandmother went home.

When Cintia woke up the next morning, she put her pillow on her bed to make it look like a sleeping body, just as she did every Sunday. She covered the pillow with the blanket and left through the window so her father would not notice she was gone.

She wasn't supposed to leave home, but she went to the little blue house.

Bruno was there.

"Hi!"

"You scared me!"

"I didn't mean to."

"Did you see the cars that came through town?" Cintia asked. "They're the ones who want to buy the house."

"Who said so?"

"Everyone."

"Maybe they're not buyers. So, are you going in?"

"No."

"Who made you change your mind? Was it Pedro?"

"You're so dumb!"

"We've got to go in, Cintia. Come on, we have to try! We've wanted to do this for so long. It's our last chance. If we don't go in now, we'll be sorry for the rest of our lives."

Cintia didn't dare, though she badly wanted to.

"It's not blue yet."

"There's still five days to go."

"It's always the same. We watch it for a whole year and one morning we wake up and it's turned blue. Do you suppose a fairy touches it with a little wand?" she wondered.

"No, I don't think it's the fairies. My mother says that someone paints it in the middle of the night. But we have to go in, Cintia. Otherwise we'll never know what's hidden inside."

"Grandmother says it's magic."

They looked at each other, their eyes saying things they couldn't speak out loud.

If only he hadn't invited that girl from out of town.

If only she hadn't said yes to Pedro.

"Let's go in, Cintia."

"Wait! Look, a car is coming!"

"Quick, let's hide! Here, behind the well."

The car parked. Two people got out.

"Grandmother told me not to come. I should have listened to her."

"Relax," he said and hugged her.

They stood very close to each other. He noticed she had a bruise.

"How did you get that?" he said.

"I fell."

"Off your bike?"

"Yes."

"Can I ask you something?"

"Yes."

"Would you like to come to the dance with me?"

She stayed like that, without moving, leaning on his shoulder. She was hoping the men in the car would never leave. Or at least that they would stay a long time so she could stay close to Bruno. He hardly ever hugged.

They both felt a tickling in their stomachs, like butterflies up and down their bellies. Love feels very much like fear. But any fear Cintia had disappeared when Bruno put his arms around her. She felt perfectly happy, perfectly complete.

The visitors got out of the car. They were carrying a gadget that they kept placing on the patio and the veranda. They were whispering.

Cintia and Bruno remained hidden, not moving. The men approached the well.

"Are you sure there's a treasure here?"

"Yes, sir," answered the other man. It sounded like the mayor himself.

The men in black came closer to their hiding place. Silently, Cintia started to cry. Tears slid down her cheeks. Bruno picked up a stone. He waited. Then he hurled it at the roof.

The pigeons flew out of their loft. Their flight sounded like thunder.

"What was that, chief?"

"I don't know."

"They say this house is haunted. We'd better get out of here."

"Don't be stupid," said the mayor. "It's only the wind."

The dust from the flying birds soon hit Cintia's nose, making her sneeze. Bruno covered her mouth with a hand full of dirt. He always had dirty hands and nails.

The men were still suspicious.

"Someone's here."

"I told you, chief. We'd better leave and come back tomorrow."

"Wait. Let's take a look."

The mayor came closer to the well.

Cintia thought her heart would leap out of her mouth. Bruno held her by the shoulders. Crouching down, they moved around the well as the mayor circled it.

Everything seemed to be happening in slow motion. Cintia decided not to give Bruno an answer about the dance until he asked her a second time. She hadn't waited this long in vain. She hadn't said yes to that clumsy Pedro for nothing.

THE TREASURE

In less than the blink of an eye, a rumor started making the rounds in Azul about a treasure the owners of the little house had buried there. No one knew more than that. They didn't even know who had started the rumor.

After their big scare at the little blue house, Cintia and Bruno didn't know what to think, but they were determined to keep investigating. At the station and the butcher shop, at the bakery and the grocery store, everyone was busy talking about the treasure.

With their big scare and all the commotion that followed, Bruno did not ask her again to go to the dance with him, though Cintia kept waiting for him to ask a second time.

There were different explanations of what was happening. Some said that the person interested in buying the house was the mayor himself, hiding behind a false buyer in order to get his hands on the treasure. Others said that the little blue house was being claimed by a descendant of Manuel Iraola, its former owner, and that he himself had put it up for sale.

Cintia could not sleep at night thinking about the little blue house being torn down and replaced with a factory. Lying awake, she imagined the magical place razed by bulldozers that would level the earth and turn it into farm land.

For her that quiet place had links to a whole chain of memories. It was there that Bruno had read many poems to her. Though not as often as Cintia, he also borrowed books from Don Simón, carrying them to the house in his bicycle basket so he could share them with her.

> *I like for you to be still: it's as though you were absent,*
> *and you do not hear me far away and my voice does not touch you.*
> *It seems as though your eyes had flown away*
> *and it seems that a kiss had sealed your mouth.*

He had read those lines to her and she couldn't stop thinking about them.

> *As all things are filled with my soul*

THE LITTLE BLUE HOUSE

you emerge from the things, filled with my soul.
You are like my soul, a butterfly of dream,
and you are like the word Melancholy.

Some lines in Neruda's book of poems had been
marked with red pencil, like these ones:

So that you will hear me
my words
sometimes grow thin
as the tracks of the gulls on the beaches.

Could Don Simón have made those markings? If
so, for whom?

Cintia and Bruno shared their books and read-
ings without letting any of the boys in town know.
The others made fun of boys who read. Bruno loved
reading to Cintia and Cintia loved to have Bruno
read to her, but no one had to know about it. Boys,
were not in the least romantic and got everything
wrong anyway.

For Cintia, the abandoned house was a safe place
filled with happy memories, mostly love stories.
There was something that connected her to the
place – the chains of poetry, magic and fate. And
perhaps there was something more, something she
could not understand. Perhaps her passion for this
place had been passed on by her grandmother.

Grandmother Pina also loved that house, more than anyone could imagine.

Cintia put her memories aside and decided to find out if there was really a treasure inside. She told Grandmother what she had heard from behind the well. Pina didn't scold her, but she did tell her that it was dangerous to keep going to the house. To tell the truth, she sounded like a broken record. If her father found out, he would punish her. In fact, she was always being punished, and she was used to it, though one should never have to get used to such a thing.

"Cintia, please promise me that you will not go back there."

Cintia was silent.

"Cintia…"

So Cintia promised. She had no choice.

Just in case, though, she kept her toes crossed.

She was different, not like the other girls. The absence of her mother had brought her close to her grandmother, and her father's bad temper had caused her to live inside herself. She was embarrassed about her father and didn't want the town to know that he mistreated her. So whenever she had bruises she said that she had fallen off her bicycle, even though, sooner or later, everyone in town found out the truth. Inside she felt ashamed, but she thought that if she told the truth, people would not love her. Besides, for reasons that were almost secret, she never said bad things about her father. She wished he were different, yes, but she never spoke about what went on inside her house.

She didn't know what to do to change her situation. She didn't know a way out of her life. Yet, something told her that a change for the better was about to take place, and that it was somehow connected to the little blue house. In the meantime, she had to bear things as they were.

Grandmother Pina's stories and the stories she heard on the radio helped Cintia make up her own stories. And then there were her dreams. Could she ever dream!

She wanted to be like Jo in *Little Women*. She wished she had a family like Jo's, even if Jo's father was away at war. It was better to have a good father away in combat than a bad father who stayed home. Maybe she thought this because of how her life was. In any case, more than anything, she wished she had sisters. She loved stories about large families. That's why she read and reread those novels and hated it when they ended. While she was reading, she could believe that she was in another world, but once she had finished a book, the story was over and she had to begin reading a new one just to survive.

She also liked the stories about Ailín that she heard over the radio, but she wondered whether they were real or made up.

Why didn't she think of it before? She should be paying more attention to the voice on the radio. It sounded almost magical, like her grandmother's voice when she told her stories. That voice must know something about what had happened, because it spoke about the past.

Going to Don Simón's bookstore made her feel happy, too. She wanted to be like him. To have so many books was like having a treasure, and one should always wish for treasures.

On Sunday night everyone in Azul listened to the stories. The rest of the people in town found it easier to listen to stories than to read them.

Cintia lay on her bed and got ready to listen.

LEGEND 4

Ailín told Don Manuel and Joaquín about the origins of the hill next to the pond.

The people of Ailín's tribe would fish and hunt for food on the plain. They would also look for seeds inside the fruit so they could spread them over the land.

This is why when Ailín and her people fled from those who wanted to kill them and arrived in the new land, the men of the tribe had brought seeds from their former lands. They carried bags that contained brown seed-pods as large as castanets.

The seeds came from a rare tree and lay inside those castanets, which opened into halves. The secret lay in opening them up and leaving them alone and free for the wind to spread the seeds and sow them wherever they fell.

The trees that grew out of those seeds were jacaranda trees. The jacaranda trees grew on a hill. But the *trees did not bloom. Ailín thought this was because their time had not yet come.*

In the beginning one tree grew next to the other, their gnarled trunks pushing up quickly. The branches soon multiplied, were covered with fine leaves and rose up to the sky. Almost all those who watched them grow were certain that the trees would bloom. Yet the years went by and the jacaranda flowers did not appear.

Blooming does not always happen as planned. There are times when it is delayed and there are times when it doesn't happen at all.

Ailín was certain that the jacaranda trees were not blooming because their time had not yet come.

INTEREST

Monday morning. Cintia's father was looking at a map when Cintia walked into the kitchen. María was not there. Cintia stood looking at him from the doorway.

She had mixed feelings about this man who beat her but who was also her father. She did not know whether she should ask him something, say hello, or just go back to her room and close the door behind her. She did not know whether she could leave through the front door, as normal people do, or whether she should go out the window. Maybe it was better to just stay invisible.

Her father did not notice her standing there because he was concentrating on what was in front of him on the table. So Cintia leaned against the wall and slid down to the floor. She sat there, practically under the table, playing with the long tablecloth.

She heard María come in and close the door. Now she had no choice but to remain completely hidden under the table. It was a very large table. She was able to hide at one end, while her father sat at the other. She could see their feet.

"Hi," María said.

Juan did not answer. Cintia heard María place something on the kitchen table.

"María, we're going to be rich very soon," said Juan.

Cintia saw María's feet move close to her father's. Her heart was bursting. Better not to think about what would happen if her father discovered her under the table. She hadn't hidden there on purpose!

María had already heard about the treasure. The whole town was a cauldron boiling with the news. Just to be safe, she said nothing.

Juan was euphoric.

"Hurry up and bring me some beer. See, here's the map Eduardo gave me. They've already started digging holes in that dump. Who would have thought there was a treasure in there? We have to be careful, though. The mayor says this treasure belongs to the town hall, and he offered me fifty percent if I help him find it. And you will help me, María."

Cintia didn't know what María was doing. All

she could see were her feet next to her father's. She watched as María lifted one heel, then the other, shifting her weight. Her father's feet remained firmly planted on the floor.

Cintia had almost stopped breathing. Her heart was racing.

"We have to get to the treasure before the heirs of that damned house arrive."

Cintia felt like she was choking. How could she get out of here? She was afraid they would find her.

She saw María's feet approach the fridge and the fridge door open and close. Then the feet went back to her father, then to the sideboard and back to the table. Cintia could tell by the sounds that she was putting down a glass.

"Juan," María said suddenly, while she poured him some beer. "Are you sure the mayor will share the treasure with you?"

There was a dangerous silence. Cintia heard her father put one hand on the table.

"How dare you have doubts about my friend?"

"People are saying the strangest things around town, Juan... "

"What are they saying? Tell me, what are they saying?"

Cintia saw her father stand up. The glass smashed against the floor and beer spilled everywhere.

This could be the end. If either one bent down, she would be discovered.

"Don't you ever repeat to me what you hear in town," Juan said to María, his feet now very close to hers. Stepping over the broken glass, he left the kitchen. María went into the pantry to get the broom, and Cintia took advantage of the opportunity to go and lock herself in her room. She could hardly believe she was safe. She couldn't believe the terrible things she had heard.

She thought about her mother. Once again she wondered if her mother had abandoned her because she could no longer stand her father. But in that case, she would have taken Cintia with her. And she hadn't.

ABSENCE

Cintia spent the rest of the day in her room. She thought a lot about her mother. There were things she couldn't understand. She also thought about her father, her grandmother, the treasure and then her grandmother again.

She didn't even feel like reading, and when she couldn't read, it meant that things were really bad.

Bruno had sent her a letter. The letter was a kind of summary of what they had talked about behind the well at the little blue house. Bruno explained that he had never invited Julián's cousin to the dance, and he begged her not to go with Pedro. He wrote that he wanted them to go together because he wasn't interested in doing anything without her.

Cintia answered that she was happy that he had cleared up things between them, that she couldn't tell him earlier because the car had appeared. She did not say that she could not do anything without him, either. There was no reason to make him feel that good.

She fell asleep thinking about Bruno and reliving their conversations.

In spite of everything that had gone on that day, that night was a happy one. Nothing could spoil the happiness she felt when Bruno told her he would go to the dance with her. She couldn't stop thinking about him. Her head was alive with him. She heard his voice, she could even smell him. She had read his letter fifteen times, and now she held it against her heart. She decided she would hold it close all night. She told herself that if she let it go, then someone would find out her secret.

THE DANCE

The time remaining until the dance felt like an eternity to Cintia, even though she was no longer confined to the house. Her father was focusing all his attention on finding the treasure, and he spent most of his time with the mayor now. This made things easier for Cintia, for María, and for Grandmother.

Saturday night. Finally it was the day of the dance. The moon came out.

Cintia had decided to find out for herself what had become of Ailín, while everyone in town was getting ready, putting on their best clothes. They were all planning to listen to the radio before heading off to the dance hall. Nothing would stop them from listening to the regular radio broadcast.

LEGEND 5

Don Manuel had to go back to Spain with his son for a time. He asked Ailín to come with them but she would not. She had decided to stay at the house.

The days felt endless to Ailín. She made dolls out of clay and rags to give to little girls who came to Capybara Pond. She wrote and wrote in her free time. She also spent hours on end near the pond watching the herons dive into the water and picking reeds to decorate the house.

It was about that time that Joaquín began to write letters telling her how much he missed her. She also missed him and remembered the moments they had shared together. He sent her poems and in one letter spoke of his wish, now a promise, that upon his return they would get married. He explained how the distance had made him understand that there was more than *friendship linking them, that nothing interested him if she was not by his side.*

Ailín felt the same, but she could not give him an answer. She could not forget the oath she had made to her parents. She could not betray her ancestors.

For a serious woman like herself, a promise was everything. She was now torn between her wish and her duty. There was no one she could talk to, and she could see no solution.

THE RADIO

There were still forty-five minutes to go before ten o'clock, when the club would open its doors to the whole town. Bruno was at home dressing for the big event.

Shaken by the story she had just heard, Cintia got on her bicycle, her white dress and the ribbon around her waist fluttering in the wind. The cold wind hurt her face. She pedaled along, letting go of the handlebars to button up her white overcoat. Grandmother Pina had knit it especially for the occasion.

She rode toward the radio station. She wanted to find out once and for all who that voice belonged to. She would find out everything there was to know about Ailín, too.

The night air was freezing cold. Just as she reached the building, a woman was closing the radio station door behind her. She wore a long overcoat, and her head was wrapped in a scarf.

"Hey!" Cintia shouted. "Wait a minute!"

The person turned around to look at Cintia. Then she started to run away. Cintia pedaled even harder to catch up with her.

"Hey! Don't go!" she shouted.

The person bent down and picked up something from the ground. Cintia braked hard and stopped. She thought the person was going to attack her. Out of habit she stood there on guard, ready to defend herself.

The streetlights were very dim. The person started to walk away. Cintia pedaled until she caught up to her.

"I need to know about Ailín, about the little blue house!" she yelled.

She heard something drop just as the person stepped off the sidewalk onto the road. She stopped her bicycle and looked around on the ground.

It was a key. Had the person dropped it on purpose or did it just fall?

When she looked up, the person was gone.

Suddenly Cintia realized that it was the key to the radio station!

She tried the key in the lock a thousand times before the door to the station finally opened. Then she went in, shaking with fear and cold.

It was dark. The room was smaller than a bathroom. Only a table and a chair were visible in the moonlight. On the table was a notebook.

Could these be the stories? Why would the person leave them behind? What light could she use to read by?

Everything was so quiet. She decided to stop asking herself so many questions. She left quickly, putting the notebook in the basket of her bike. As usual, she had books in the basket so no one would suspect that she was carrying a secret – her father, least of all.

She began pedaling. Instead of turning the corner to go home to put the notebook away, however, the bike took her in the direction of the little blue house. On the way there she ran into Bruno.

"Cintia, where are you going? We have to go to the dance first so everyone will see us. Then we can make our escape."

"Fine, but no matter what, at midnight we're going over to the little blue house. I have to tell you something very important. It can't wait."

"It's a deal."

They turned back and went to the dance.

The whole town was there. Grandmother Pina in a green dress, Don Simón in a brown suit, María dressed in a long yellow gown. Luckily, Cintia's father had decided not to go. He hated parties.

Everyone knew that he was at the mayor's house

playing cards. Behind the town hall was a house that had once belonged to the mayor's guards, where they went to gamble and play poker. Many townspeople had lost everything they owned there – their houses, even their wives.

Who knows, Cintia thought, my father could be scheming with the mayor about how to find the treasure. She suddenly realized that her father had barely been at home over the past few days.

If only Pina were her mother. Nobody in this world loved her as much as her grandmother Pina.

But Grandmother did not love Cintia's mother. She didn't even try to see her. She had never forgiven her for not leaving a note when she left. Even if her life with Cintia's father had been hell, she should have taken her daughter with her.

Cintia had always wanted someone to adopt her. She had often thought that the best medicine for her sorrows would have been if her grandmother told her a story in which she was the main character. It would be a story in which someone would say that her parents weren't her real parents after all, and that she was free to set out to find her true mother and father.

Everyone in town was dressed up and in the mood to party. The hall opened its doors to the people of Azul and the neighboring towns.

By midnight, the band was playing *cumbias* and

everyone was on the dance floor. Cintia and Bruno were chatting in the hall where everyone could see them. Bruno wanted to know what Cintia had to tell him, but he couldn't ask her until they were alone.

Later they slipped out of the club without being noticed, one leaving from the back of the hall, the other from the front. There was no one outside. Everyone was at the dance.

"Are you ready?"

"Are you?"

They took the dirt road, crossed the railroad tracks and turned in the direction of the little blue house.

"Now will you tell me?"

"When we get to the little blue house. It's too dangerous here."

For the villagers back at the club, the night was quickly turning into a most exciting time. Dances usually lasted until the morning. The moment dawn began to turn the sky pink, Don Darwin's wife would serve everyone hot chocolate and *churros*.

CHANCE MEETING

As they pedaled toward the little blue house, Bruno suddenly said, "Cintia, can you forgive me?"

"Forgive what?"

"Forgive me for making you mad so many times."

"Don't you like Julián's cousin?"

"She's conceited, like all those women. Julián insisted I ask her to the dance and then she told all her friends that I had already invited her. Cintia… "

"What?"

"I really like being with you."

Cintia blushed. It was cold and dark and Bruno couldn't see her. He was blushing, too.

They kept quiet until they arrived at the house. After they hid their bicycles, they walked slowly over to the well. The crickets sang their usual song. Every now and then a horse neighed, distracting them a little. They could hear the music coming from the dance in the distance. They stayed close to each other, but not because they were afraid.

It occurred to Bruno that Cintia never noticed how his eyes filled with emotion every time he saw her, how his hands shook when he hugged her and how he was dying to kiss her.

Cintia, on the other hand, thought that he never noticed how her breathing became shorter when he took her hand, how her belly rose and fell when he whispered to her.

The moon was full, very full. There was no danger of being caught tonight unless Cintia's father sent someone to the dance to look for her. That had been known to happen, and if it did, they would notice she wasn't there, and there would be trouble.

"And if your mom finds out that you're not there?" she asked Bruno.

"I'll pay for it, just like you."

Cintia didn't say anything because she knew that what would happen to her would never happen to Bruno. She was too ashamed to say that her father hit her.

"Cintia, before you say anything, I want to ask you something. Will you be my girlfriend?"

She did not answer. She was speechless. Behind them the choir of frogs and crickets started yet again. A *tero* lost in the winter night let out a heart-rending sound. The dogs in town barked in unison.

"The treasure…" said Cintia.

"You didn't answer my question."

"I can't. I'm too embarrassed."

"Then don't say anything. But would you mind if I kissed you?"

She closed her eyes and he drew closer.

They were about a millimeter apart when a car drove up the dirt road to the house. They stayed in their hiding place, waiting for someone to get out. The first person was the driver, a man dressed in black – an out-of-towner, obviously, as there were no drivers in Azul. Then, to their surprise, a second man, smoking a pipe, got out of the right side of the car and walked around to the other side to help a fat woman out of the back seat.

She was wearing a scarf around her head, and she walked in a familiar way. She reminded Cintia of someone. The man was wearing a hat. The woman wore a long overcoat, like the person at the radio station.

Cintia couldn't see their faces or make out any colors. She and Bruno remained motionless, praying that no one would notice their bicycles.

The man led the woman to the door while the driver began to dig a hole by the well.

"Wait a minute," said the man. "Did you hear that?"

"Don't be afraid, dear. It's just the wind."

Those voices, Cintia thought. They sounded so familiar, but she couldn't place them.

"That voice!" said Bruno.

They were still holding hands.

Cintia was starting to feel afraid.

"Something strange is going on here."

"It's the woman from the radio station!" Cintia whispered.

"What do you mean? It's Don Simón!"

"But how can it be Don Simón? I didn't have the chance to tell you, Bruno. I saw that woman at the radio station!"

When the man lit a match to light his tobacco, they recognized Don Simón immediately.

"He's looking for the treasure."

"And I thought that he was honest," Cintia said.

Suddenly the driver brought the car closer and shed light on the treasure seekers.

"It's Grandmother Pina! How can it be?"

"Who's there?"

In a few words Cintia told Bruno what had happened at the radio station.

"The woman from the radio station is – "

That's when the driver came out with the flashlight and found them. They were embarrassed and surprised, but they didn't let go of each other's hands.

"You? Here?"

It was all over.

DISCOVERY

"Please, we can explain. Grandmother, don't scold us. It's just that – "

"What are you doing here?"

"Don Simón! Cintia can explain everything," Bruno said.

"You, always so brave, you..."

The two old people faced the children. All four were in shock. All four were trying to explain with their eyes what they could not yet express in words.

Cintia had so many questions. All her doubts combined to form a long chain, like a train slowly pulling an endless number of wagons.

A long silence settled between them – a silence that seemed to last forever. It was a heavy silence full of uncertainty. But, like all silences no matter how strong, it was eventually broken.

"You must promise that you will keep this secret."

"Of course."

"We swear."

Grandmother looked at Cintia, who had once sworn she would never go back to the little house.

"Grandma, I swear on my mother – "

"Not necessary, child, not necessary."

The chest they had just dug up was on the ground in front of them. Cintia sat down to see what they would do. Don Simón smoked his pipe and gave orders.

"Not a word about this to anyone," he said. Then he looked at the driver. "Take the children back to the dance. Everything must go on as usual. We'll talk tomorrow."

"No, Grandma. Tell him to let us stay just a little longer. Please, we won't tell!"

"But what if your father finds out?"

"Pina."

"Yes?"

"The chest."

"What's the matter with the chest?"

"It's blue."

Grandmother Pina and Don Simón were silent. Bruno and Cintia understood nothing.

"Here's what we'll do. Let's take the chest to your place, Pina. We have to leave now."

Pedro was a driver from the city that Pina had hired. He put the blue chest in the trunk next to the bicycles. As soon as they reached town, Bruno and Cintia got out of the car and rode back to the dance.

They wanted to be alone and not be bothered by anyone. They wanted dawn to come so the dance would be over. Cintia told Bruno what she had seen at the radio station. Even if no one had said anything, some things were finally clear. Her grandmother Pina and the woman at the radio station were the same person. And yet the mystery surrounding everything else remained.

It was all so complicated.

"What if we go to Grandmother Pina's house?"

So many questions were in their minds, it was impossible for them to sit still.

"They're going to scold us, Cintia."

"And what are we going to do if we stay here?"

"I don't know. But, how come your grandmother never said anything?"

"I don't understand."

Night was turning into dawn. Nobody was out in the street because it was too cold. Cintia and Bruno were still amazed and somehow delighted by this unexpected surprise.

"Cintia."

"What?"

"I think we were interrupted when I was just about to kiss you."

Cintia did not answer as she put her cold hands over her hot red cheeks.

MORE NEWS

Sunday morning. The town was in shock when they woke up to the news. The mayor was furious. Someone had dug a hole at the little blue house the night of the dance.

The scoundrels had taken the treasure!

The chief of police began an investigation. Cintia and Bruno were back at their own houses and pretended not to know a thing about what had happened.

"Did you hear about the treasure, you little brat?" yelled Cintia's father. "They got to it ahead of us!"

Cintia stood in the corner by the chest of drawers where the family pictures were displayed, holding her head between her hands. She couldn't tell whether her father was going to hit her, but she protected herself just in case. Her father tended to say things that didn't have much to do with what had caused his fury in the first place. When he got mad about something, it was as if he took his anger out of a suitcase. He rummaged around to find events that had made him furious years before and piled them up, one on top of the other, in a tower of grievances.

Cintia didn't like to hear the things her father said. She would cover her ears without him noticing so as not to irritate the angry man even more.

But it didn't matter how well she covered her ears. The words filtered through. Ugly words have no respect. They squeeze their way in, no matter what.

"I don't know what to do with you, Cintia. You'd better get out of my sight for a while. To think that I had promised my friend I would find the treasure. Now he's going to kill me."

Cintia ran over to Grandmother Pina's house. No one was there. Then she went to Don Simón's. She found Bruno at the door.

"Hi!"

"Hi!"

"Did you have a good time last night?"

"Yes."

"Have you heard anything? What are people saying?"

"We have to be careful. Let's not say a word."

"Grandmother Pina is gone and so is Don

Simón. Where did they go? What have you got in there, Cintia?"

"It's the notebook with the legends."

"Where did you get it?"

"It was on the table at the radio station. The writing is my grandmother's. I've had the notebooks in my bicycle basket the whole time. I took them out when they put our bikes in the trunk. Didn't you notice?"

"No."

"Grandmother did, but she didn't say anything. Are we going to read them?"

"It's cold out here. Let's go to my place," Bruno said.

There was no one at Bruno's house either. It was Sunday, and even though everyone had been at the dance the night before, the weekly trip to the cemetery was not canceled.

The morning was cold and they were both sleepy.

"A cup of coffee and milk will wake us up."

It was a winter morning with a heavy fog. The street was barely visible. The fog covered all of Azul in a cold, thick white mist, as if it was protecting the town from some rare event

"Did you listen to last night's legend?" Cintia asked Bruno.

"Yes, I heard it."

They started reading what they had so often heard told by the storytelling voice on the radio. They hoped they would find the explanation to everything that was going on. The legends might hold a secret.

Cintia and Bruno loved secrets, especially now that they were on the verge of uncovering one. There were other secrets to be uncovered, too, but for that they had a long road to walk down together.

LEGEND 6

One day, after many unanswered love letters, Joaquín sent a man from Europe to bring Ailín to him. But the beautiful native girl said she would not go. She could not betray her parents. The man took her message back to Joaquín, and they say the poor lad died right then from a broken heart.

Don Manuel wrote to Ailín to tell her what had happened. He described the tragic death of his son in the smallest detail, and as a writer he did it so well, expressing his sorrow in such an eloquent manner, that before she finished the letter, Ailín died as well.

A rumor circulated in the village that the letter Ailín had received was poisoned. She stopped moving while she read it, and that was how they found her, still and lifeless. Nobody dared to touch the letter, so they buried her with the letter in her hands.

This tragedy happened on November 27. She was buried that evening. On the morning of November 28, *the entire hill was covered with blue flowers for the first time. And on that same day, the house – the white house that Don Manuel had built many years before – turned blue.*

Everyone was surprised to see the house change color overnight. They said that blue was the color for lovers, and that to symbolize the lovers' separation, the walls of the house had taken on the love Joaquín and Ailín had been unable to express.

The color blue took over everything in the house. If you looked through the windows, you could see blue curtains, blue sewing boxes, little blue tables and blue lamps.

The village was abuzz with talk of the blue house. But, in the meantime, a most curious event had taken place. The house that had dawned all blue the day before was blue no longer.

The days came and went, months turned into years, and everyone kept talking about the blue house.

Much later, Don Manuel came back, sad and alone, carrying the burden of his bitter memories. He gathered everything Ailín and Joaquín had written and put it all away, tied up with a blue ribbon. No one ever found out where he had hidden the papers.

The village grew into a town that came to be known as Azul, and from that day on, people have always referred to the house as la casita azul *– "the little blue house."*

BIG LUNCH

Cintia and Bruno were speechless.

"Let's keep reading," Cintia said.

"There's your grandmother!" Bruno cried from the window.

They grabbed their bikes and caught up with Grandmother, who was dressed in an elegant black suit.

"Grandma, where are you going?"

"Come to my place for lunch and I'll tell you. It isn't fair that you should have to wait so long to learn the truth. I can't come right now, but I would think that two intelligent young people like yourselves would have found out a few things by now anyway."

"Grandmother, aren't you going to tell us anything? It's not fair. We're dying to know."

"I'll see you at noon. Cintia, don't go back home. Don't let your father see you."

"He's furious."

"That's why. Stay with Bruno."

Noon took forever to come.

A thousand ideas crossed Cintia's mind. Both she and Bruno wanted to know what Grandmother had done with the chest. Why did she keep it? How did she know where the treasure was? What was inside? How would Cintia ever go back home? Some day she would have to, wouldn't she? Was this also part of Grandmother's plan?

The town was full of police cars. The mayor went back and forth to the little blue house. The chief of police talked through a loudspeaker.

"If they put Grandmother and Don Simón in jail, we're finished."

"And if they ask us, what will we say?"

"Nothing. We don't know a thing."

With all the excitement, it had been some time since Bruno had killed any birds. Cintia was afraid that he was about to start again. But then she noticed that he no longer carried the slingshot in his back pocket.

The sun came out in the middle of the sky. Almost at the same time as they were parking their bikes outside Grandmother Pina's house, she arrived with Don Simón.

Bruno and Cintia looked at each other. The secret was now only as far away as lunchtime. They went into Grandmother's house.

Pina went through her usual routine. She put on her apron and blew on the fire in the wood stove. She heated up the tomato sauce in one pot and in another she put the water on to boil for the spaghetti. Once it was done, she drained the spaghetti and took something from a blue bottle. She then asked all three to close their eyes.

"Blue spaghetti!" yelled Bruno.

"Is it edible?" asked the bookseller.

Cintia, by now an expert in eating blue spaghetti, winked at her grandmother.

And they ate. They even soaked their bread in the tomato sauce.

"I think we owe them an explanation," said Grandmother.

A long time ago, when I came to this town, the only person I knew was a man named Aníbal – a man who had left his country in search of a future. He had waited for me to come. He became my husband. Later on, he died. Widowed and with a little daughter, in the throes of sorrow and despair, I spoke about my suffering with an old gentleman. He was eighty-four at the time, and his name was Manuel Iraola.

He had also come from Spain, only much

earlier. He was good friends with the station master.

For a long time Manuel was like a grandfather to me. He had lost a son and a native girl that he had adopted when she was a teenager. He told me their stories to console me. He told me about his son Joaquín and Ailín, about their hopeless love. That was how I began to visit Mr. Iraola's house. Even then, the house was famous.

I was thirty-three when I met another man, two years my senior. He was Don Manuel's gardener. He was working very hard to set up a bookstore close to the railway station. That man's name was Simón. We used to go to Don Manuel's house in the afternoons to read next to the fireplace. Simón was engaged to marry a woman in the town.

Thus began a friendship that lasted many years, broken only when Don Manuel, tired and lonely, returned to his native Spain for good.

Don Manuel wanted to visit his son's grave. He could not go on living with the sorrow he felt after the death of the person he loved most in the world. I know what it means to lose a child and now I understand his sorrow. When such an absence is caused by death, the pain never goes away.

When Don Manuel left for the second and final time, he left me notebooks filled with the poetry that Joaquín had written, as well as a few romantic novels the two of them had read together. Simón and I met in the afternoons and read the books Don Manuel had left for us. Soon the whole town was gossiping about us.

A young widow and a gentleman about to get married, getting together at Don Manuel's house... It didn't look good. At that very moment we received notice that Don Manuel had died. So it was that on February 14, Saint Valentine's Day, Simón and I decided to put the treasure, the love letters and Don Manuel's last will and testament inside the chest that he kept in his basement, and thus close the house and our friendship forever.

We would have inherited the house, but Don Manuel had included a clause in his will that we were unable to comply with. Simón was to be married in just a few days, and I had to take care of my little Lilly. We couldn't go on seeing each other. So it was that we decided to bury those mementos to protect Ailín and Joaquín the way Don Manuel would have liked.

Nobody knew that we had buried the treasure. It was all so sad that we decided to try to forget about it.

Every year, on November 28, the house turns blue. The next day it's back to its usual color. Everybody knows about that. What they don't know, but must surely suspect, is that when Ruverino came to Azul, he exploited the house, creating the outings for tourists and inventing the Jacaranda Festival. We could never do anything to prevent it.

Don Manuel told us the story of Ailín and Joaquín so many times that we ended up thinking of their love as something we would have liked to experience as well. For this reason we never approved of the idea of the mayor profiting from that story. We just didn't know what to do about it.

The years went by. We never discussed the matter again. We never went back to the house.

We were the only ones who knew about the secret treasure. It was never a question of money. But with time, gossip grew and different versions of the events started to circulate and take hold.

Only when Simón became a widower, almost twenty years later, did we meet by chance at the little blue house one afternoon. We resented Ruverino's shameless actions and decided that if the situation became dangerous, we would unearth the chest. Well, seven years have passed since the promise we made to each other. You saw us digging it up and you know the rest...

The four of them were sitting at the table with the letters, books and poetry from the once-white chest spread out before them. The only unromantic thing was the dank, damp smell coming from the letters and books.

"This notebook that Ailín wrote is for you, Cintia."

"For me?"

"I know you'll take good care of it. And these recipes are for you, Bruno. Joaquín also liked to hunt for little birds."

"Grandmother..."

"Hush! No excuses,..." said Don Simón.

"What will happen to the house?"

"That's what I wanted to talk to you about," Grandmother said. "But before we go into that, you might want to read these things that are so well preserved because Simón and I wrapped them so well."

For A from J

To make a prairie it takes a clover and one bee,
One clover, and a bee,
And revery.
The revery alone will do
If bees are few.

Emily Dickinson

MORE THINGS
FROM THE CHEST

"These were the books Ailín and Joaquín used to read."

"I think I'd like this one…"

"This one is for me…"

"Now let's divide them up democratically," said Grandmother. She put *Don Quijote* to one side and *One Thousand and One Nights* on the other. Cintia couldn't see the other books she was adding to the pile with *Don Quijote*.

"Can't I have all the books?"

"Cintia, that's not very generous of you…"

For Joaquín

STRINGED PARTRIDGES
Tie six partridges with sturdy string.
Fry two onions in very hot oil.
Cut up two carrots and two celery stalks.

Add two heads of garlic and some vinegar.

PICKLED HARE
Place one hare under briskly running water until
    it turns white.
Place it in a mixture of laurel leaf, broth and lard.
Let it marinate for two days before roasting.

April 11, 1955

Dear Pina and Simón:
    I hope old age won't have killed me by the
time you read this. Dear friends, I have written
my last will with my own hand, and as I don't
have any heirs, I wish the house to be yours. You
are the ones who have shown me that there is
meaning to life.
    Should other heirs be forced on you, I disin-
herit them. I have named an executor so that
my will may stand.
    Forgive me for being so audacious. I simply
want the house to be yours, and for that to happen you will have to grant the wish of a ninety-
four-year-old man you will never see again. I
want you to be together until the end.
                                    Manuel Iraola

QUESTIONS

Sunday afternoon.

"Grandma, can I ask about… you two?"

"It's a very long story."

"Children," Don Simón said. "There are things you will learn about in good time."

"You may have guessed already," said Grandmother Pina. "The executor named by Don Manuel died. But his son has kept in touch with us. Tomorrow everything will be resolved. Cintia, don't go home yet."

"But if I don't go, my father will come for me, Grandma."

She and Bruno stayed at Grandmother Pina's house until the evening, though both Grandmother and Don Simón had to leave. Cintia didn't know what to do. Should she stay there? Should she go home? Should she run away?

The magic voice spoke on the radio that night, as if nothing out of the ordinary had taken place in Azul.

LEGEND 7

Some say that a gentleman from Spain witnessed a great love story in a village that was once founded by natives. The love he witnessed could not prosper because fate intervened. After that there was another love story. This love was not allowed to prosper, either.

Poetry linked the two stories.

The man had seen the unhappiness of love that was cut short and wanted his house to be a witness to true love.

They say that the willows around the pond of that house bend down because of the weight of the sadness of those times. When people talk about those willows, they say they weep.

In the end, time took care of these problems, and the twin souls who could not be united in their youth at last came together. Time also helped rid the town of evildoers.

The town of Azul celebrated the downfall of the man who had exploited the region's most beautiful myth. This was a man who invented phony heirs and salespeople in order to keep the money and the house to himself.

The lovers triumphed over those who had been blinded by material ambition. The town of Azul recovered its magic and its honesty, but lost one of its main Sunday attractions in the process.

The train no longer came to town, as no one wanted to visit the little blue house once the secret was revealed. No one cared once there was no profit to be made from the stories. Azul was left without a train but returned to its tranquil, peaceful ways.

Azul was forgotten by everyone, but the town won one big victory. For the first time, people were able to choose who would govern them.

Hope returned to the town of Azul and love returned to the little blue house, because love does not die. Love lives on and lovers wait. Many years had to pass before the two lovers could face the rest of the world and bring a happy ending to the little blue house. Or was it a happy beginning?

"That's Grandmother!" Cintia said to Bruno. "She doesn't have the notebook because I have it. She's making it up as she goes along, forecasting the future of Azul. I better not think about anything else and just wait. This is exhausting!"

"Don't go to your house tonight. You should stay here at your grandmother's. But I have to leave."

"I can't do that, Bruno, and you know it."

"Then I'll go with you."

When Cintia arrived home after that exhausting day, her father was waiting for her.

She got off her bike. Bruno waited on the sidewalk.

Cintia's father was angry. It was very late.

"Bye, Bruno, I'll see you later!"

"Are you sure you want me to go?"

Cintia did not answer.

"I told you not to leave the house, you little brat. Where have you been?" shouted her father.

Bruno stayed on his bicycle, waiting.

"And you, go home!"

Cintia's father pushed her into the house. Bruno left, worried. Should he tell Grandmother Pina? He thought about it and then took off faster than the wind.

Cintia's father removed his belt, grabbed it by the buckle and wrapped it around his fist three times. She ran to the corner where the portraits were. Her father followed her. She tried to avoid him as long as she could. She bent down, covered her head, folded her fingers together. She covered her ears with her forearms and raised her elbows to protect her face. She curled up into a ball. She prayed for the blows not to come.

Her tears came out like waterfalls.

"Don't hit me anymore, please, Daddy," she begged, crying. "Don't hit me anymore!"

In the meantime, Bruno had followed his instincts and told Grandmother what was happening. She arrived with the police as Cintia was screaming, "I want my mother!"

Grandmother hugged her very tightly, kissing her over and over. When Cintia was finally able to listen once more, she told her reassuringly, "Together we'll find your mother." Then she embraced her again.

They both knew that hugs could cure people who had been treated badly. And this was something Cintia had to know. From now on, whenever those horrible memories came back to her, she would ask for a hug. But not from just anyone. It had to be someone who loved her a lot.

Grandmother packed some of Cintia's things and took her granddaughter back to her house.

LATER

J ustice finally came to Azul. María agreed to testify about the mistreatment Cintia had suffered. Grandmother obtained the ownership of the little blue house.

The son of Don Manuel's lawyer agreed that Don Eduardo Ruverino did not own a license for use of the house as a tourist attraction. With the help of witnesses, they managed to jail him for abuse of power. People found their courage and testified against the criminals.

Cintia's father also went to jail because he was so closely linked to Ruverino. His situation was complicated not just by his connections to the mayor, but by his violence, especially toward his daughter. Others also ended up in jail. Fortunately, they were sent to the city jail and not to the one in Azul.

After that, the Jacaranda Festival was not celebrated the way it had been before. The days of the tours to the little blue house organized for profit by the mayor were over. Paid trips to the cemetery also ended.

On the morning of November 27, the whole town of Azul arrived at the little house. There were very important reasons for this year's celebration. Cintia and Grandmother were at the door. Don Simón and Bruno greeted everyone at the gate. There were blue balloons in all the windows in honor of the day. The band played and the soft aroma of the blue jacaranda flowers rained like mist on the faces of the citizens of Azul, who had come to breathe in the perfumed air for the first time in so many years.

They had restored the house and painted it white. For the first time since people could remember, free elections for mayor were held. Three candidates had run campaigns over four months. The winner was an elderly gentleman that Don Simón knew very well.

Don Eduardo Ruverino, his wife and their henchmen would be in jail for a good long while.

"This house is no longer abandoned," said Grandmother to the crowd. "It will be a library, a radio station and the town archive. That's the reason for this celebration. With the books that were in the house, plus Cintia's, Bruno's, Don Simón's and my own, this place can become one of our community's major attractions. This deserves to be celebrated. Blue spaghetti and mandarin orange juice for everyone!"

So by losing a tourist attraction, the people of Azul gained knowledge of their own history.

Simón and Pina were married, paying no attention to the gossip coming from the town's older women. Don Simón no longer needed to share his store and now rented the whole thing to Clarita.

At the entrance to the little house they put up a sign that read:

Don Manuel Iraola, Azul Cultural Center

Cintia helped transplant her grandmother's jasmine bush. Many of the things that had belonged to Ailín were placed in one of the rooms. They say that the weeping willows next to the pond straightened up a little in order to be more like the jacaranda trees.

"Grandmother, when Don Manuel sent you the letter, was Don Simón married?"

"Cintia, I want you to know that Don Manuel believed in true love. He could not accept that people who loved one another should be apart. He never understood why Ailín and Joaquín did not fulfill their love. He didn't understand our love, either. But Simón had given his word to the woman he was engaged to, so he married her. I would never have accepted his breaking the engagement. Do you see what I mean?"

"Well, yes, but you don't have to get mad. With so many secrets, I just thought that maybe the two of you had always been going out together."

THE MOST BEAUTIFUL
NIGHT IN THE WORLD

When the celebrations were over the night of November 27, the people of the town went to sleep. But Cintia and Bruno planned to stay awake until dawn to see if the house would still turn blue. Some people said it wouldn't. It was likely, they said, that all these years the mayor either painted the house, or had someone else paint it. He had taken advantage of the fact that no one was up at dawn on November 28 after all the partying. People were in no condition to go to the house until later in the morning.

Now things were different. The little house was not abandoned, and the mayor no longer took advantage of it. Instead, it was a cultural center.

Things were different now for Cintia, too. She felt free and loved. Still, she wondered just like everyone else, would the house turn blue?

At four in the morning and with Grandmother's

permission, Cintia took a flashlight and walked over to Capybara Pond. The stars looked like they were shooting toward the town, the moon was close, and the spring dew was starting to rise.

She was happy with her grandmother's decision. She was going to love living here in the house that had played such an important role in her life. At the same time, she understood that she could never be completely happy. She missed her mother, and her father, too. Despite everything, she loved them both. But the love she got from her grandmother, Don Simón and Bruno helped to heal her and made up for the love she was missing.

Pina always reminded her that Bruno had known what her father was about to do that ugly night. Cintia would always feel embarrassed that Bruno knew that her father hit her. It took her a while to believe it wasn't her fault. The fact that the whole town knew everything that had gone on also tormented her. But she felt proud that Bruno had saved her. And she was proud of the plan her grandmother had put together to free her from that ugly life. For could anyone doubt that Pina had led Cintia's father and the mayor into a trap with the radio station, the stories, the treasure, the gossip?

Cintia lay on the rock and made drawings in the sky with her flashlight. Suddenly a flurry of pigeons fluttering their wings made her aware of someone else's presence.

Someone was walking toward the pond.

"Hi."

"Hi."

"May I keep you company?"

"Of course."

This time his arrival hadn't frightened her.

"I love you very much," said Bruno, caressing her face.

Cintia felt the uneasiness in her body turn into a tingling sensation.

There were no more interruptions. On this, the most important night of the year for the people of Azul, Bruno took her face in his hands.

"You know what?" Cintia said.

"Don't say a thing," answered Bruno. "There's no need." Then he kissed her, and they were silent while a soft breeze washed over their faces.

Five minutes passed.

"Bruno, I need to tell you something else."

"Whatever you want, Cintia, but nothing will change our agreement. From now on we will always be together. Is that what you want?"

Then he kissed her again.

And while he did, the little house began, very slowly, to turn blue...

GLOSSARY

Capybara – A large aquatic South American mammal. An excellent swimmer, it is the largest rodent in the world.

Churros – A donut-like pastry.

Cumbias – Instrumental dance music with few lyrics, originating from Colombia.

Locro – A stew made from beans, meat and potatoes.

Mate – A tea typical of Argentina, traditionally drunk through a *bombilla* or metal straw.

Mazamorra – Cornmeal pudding.

Ombú – A large evergreen tree with an umbrella canopy. One of the few trees to grow on the Argentinian *pampas* or grasslands, since it can survive on very little water.

Palos borrachos – A barkless tree shaped like a bottle, with large thorns and beautiful orchid-shaped flowers.

Tero-tero – A bird that usually makes a loud noise to warn people that someone is approaching the house.